Killing Dante

A COMEDY IN TWO ACTS

by

Shannon Michal Dow
and Jan Henson Dow

SAMUEL FRENCH

FOUNDED 1830

NEW YORK HOLLYWOOD LONDON TORONTO

SAMUELFRENCH.COM

ISBN 978-0-573-66399-4   Printed in U.S.A.   #13631

IMPORTANT BILLING AND CREDIT REQUIREMENTS

All producers of *KILLING DANTE must* give credit to the Author of the Play in all programs distributed in connection with performances of the Play, and in all instances in which the title of the Play appears for the purposes of advertising, publicizing or otherwise exploiting the Play and/or a production. The name of the Author *must* appear on a separate line on which no other name appears, immediately following the title and *must* appear in size of type not less than fifty percent of the size of the title type.

KILLING DANTE was chosen for the New England Academy of Theatre's 1999 New Play Series and received a reading in New Haven, CT. The reading was directed by Ruth Beaumont and was Stage Managed by Allison DeBlasio with the following cast:

ROGER CABOT . . . . Tim O'Brien
REBECCA CABOT . . . . Sarah Caliendo
RICHARD BORMAN . . . . David Heskes
JASON STEWART . . . . John Bachelder
ABIGAIL EVANS . . . . Elizabeth Harnett
AVIS HARPINGLER . . . . Valerie Fidler
THOMAS THOMAS . . . . Chris Spence

It was also given a reading in 2000 at The Schoolhouse Theatre, Croton Falls, NY. Both were directed by Ruth Beaumont.

KILLING DANTE, also, has been a Finalist in five national playwriting competitions, including the prestigious Julie Harris Playwright Competition sponsored by the Beverly Hills Theatre Guild, The 1999 Writer's Digest Contest, and the McLaren Memorial Comedy Competition, where it was one of four Finalists which received staged readings at the Midland Community Theatre, Midland, TX.

CAST OF CHARACTERS

(In order of appearance)

ROGER CABOT - 50; a Fortune 500 company president turned bohemian painter. Has a rare condition in which he sees sounds. Always dynamic with a sharp sense of humor. Quirky in Act I; acts the calculating businessman in Act II. (Note. Synesthesia is a real neurological condition in which two senses are cross-wired.)

REBECCA CABOT - Early to mid-20's; Roger's daughter. Pretty, sweet and sincere. Initially uncertain and timid, she progressively grows more self-assured.

RICHARD BORMAN - 34; Roger's right-hand man in business and Rebecca's fiancee. Handsome and manicured. Is critical of the bohemian Roger out of Roger's presence, but more of a yes-man in his presence. Admires his mentor, Roger Cabot, and will do anything to return Roger to the conniving, calculating businessman he once was. He learns to sorely regret this ambition.

JASON STEWART - 34; a neurosurgeon hired to cure Roger. Attractive and very sincere. A former fraternity brother of Richard's. Very clumsy around the woman he loves – namely – Rebecca.

ABIGAIL EVANS - Early 40's; a tabloid journalist hired by Jason to ghostwrite his book. Attractive, good figure. Sarcastic, but a romantic underneath.

AVIS HARPINGER - 30-35; a lawyer and Jason's fiancee. Tall, slim, beautiful, self-centered, and calculating.

THOMAS THOMAS - (pronounced "toe-MAS – toe-MAS") 30's to 40's; a gay art gallery owner; friendly and delightful, but knows the bottom line.

TIME AND PLACE

A loft in New York City in the late 1990s.

COSTUMES

ROGER CABOT - In Act One he dresses in a traditional male Japanese robe and sandals. In Act Two he dresses in an expensive business suit.

REBECCA CABOT - In Act One she dresses in expensive, but understated clothes. In Act Two she wears free-flowing, brighter, more expressive clothing.

RICHARD BORMAN - An expensive business suit except when he dresses as Um-Um in Act Two, where he wears a sexy, short, red dress, a blonde wig and spike heels and carries a tiny evening bag.

JASON STEWART - Casual, but expensive clothing. In Act Two, Scene Three, dresses in khaki shirt and pants, hiking boots, an Indiana Jones hat and carries a large Indian drum slung over his shoulder.

ABIGAIL EVANS - Casual, tasteful clothing.

AVIS HARPINGER. Expensive suits consisting of a short black skirt and black jacket.

THOMAS THOMAS - Casual, trendy clothing.

THE SET

A New York City loft typical of a once industrial space now converted to a studio/living area. The walls are brick. The upstage center wall has a row of large windows. In the center is a set of French doors leading to a rooftop patio. A kitchenette area is left. Downstage right is the doorway entering into the loft from the building's hall. Upstage Left is a doorway into a room offstage.

In Act One the loft is indicative of Roger Cabot's artist lifestyle. Various canvases are stacked against the walls. The furniture consists of a number of large throw pillows and a low, narrow, black coffee table or armless and backless bench. What appears to be a modern, very uncomfortable-looking chair, is actually one of Roger's sculptures covered with a large drop cloth. An easel with a large canvas turned away from the audience is upstage right. Next to the easel is a stool, a small table with a palette, paintbrushes in a coffee can and various jars and rags. Plain drapes are drawn open on either side of the doors. A mobile of crystals hangs next to the French doors. Just visible on the patio are some rock formations of Roger's Zen rock garden.

In Act Two, the loft resembles a business office. All of Roger's artist accouterments are gone.

NOTE: The sculpture chair should resemble a chair; however, it should be very difficult for anyone to actually sit on.

To the memory of Robert Schroeder.

– JHD

and

*To my father, Louis Dow, who is proof that it's
never too late to change one's life.*

– SMD

ACT ONE

Scene One

(The New York City loft of **ROGER CABOT**. *Late one weekday afternoon.)*

(The loft is typical of a once industrial space now converted to a studio/living area. The walls are brick. The upstage center wall has a row of large windows. In the center is a set of French doors leading to a rooftop patio. Plain drapes are drawn open on either side of the doors. A mobile of crystals hangs next to the French doors. Just visible on the patio are some rock formations of Roger's Zen rock garden. A kitchenette area is left. Downstage right is the doorway entering into the loft from the building's hall. Upstage left is a doorway into a room offstage. Various canvases are stacked against the walls. The furniture consists of a number of large throw pillows and a low, narrow, black table or armless and backless bench. What appears to be a modern, very uncomfortable-looking chair, is actually one of Roger's sculptures covered with a large drop cloth. An easel with a large canvas turned away from the audience is upstage right. Next to the easel is a stool, a small table with a palette, paintbrushes in a coffee can and various jars and rags.)

(Slow Chinese MUSIC is playing.)

*(***ROGER CABOT** *is at the easel painting.)*

(He is wearing a Japanese kimono and sandals. He is dynamic and quirky with a sharp sense of humor. He has a rare condition called synesthesia in which he sees sounds.)

*(***ROGER** *is periodically distracted from his painting by a series of shapes which form in the air in correspondence*

with the music. Obviously, only he can see the shapes.)

ROGER. Dark purple triangles…Blue bubbles…Fuzzy like a peach….A burst of yellow spikes! Tiny swirls. Perfect! Right on her left breast.

(The MUSIC ends. There are several KNOCKS on the downstage right door.)

(ROGER *"sees" the knocks, speaking to himself happily as he crosses to the door to open it)* What delightful red squiggly lines! That must be her!

REBECCA. *(offstage, downstage right)* Dad?

ROGER. *(to himself:)* Rebecca?

(ROGER *peeks through the peep hole, then, speaking to himself:)* And she's brought that buffoon with her! I think I'll just hide on the patio. Maybe they'll go away.

(He quickly exits through the French doors onto the roof- top patio, closing the curtains and doors behind him.)

(REBECCA *opens the front door and enters.* **RICHARD** *enters behind her. She is dressed in expensive, but under- stated clothing. She is sweet, sincere and timid. He is dressed impeccably in an expensive suit. He is handsome and manicured and ambitious.)*

REBECCA. Dad? Are you here?

RICHARD. My God! Just look at this place! Is this the kind of place a man who's the envy of the business world should live in? *(looking around in alarm at the loft)* What happened to those Louis XVI chairs your father col- lected? And that Empire dining table? And the Chippendale lowboys? Don't tell me he's sold them all! *(after* **REBECCA** *doesn't answer:)* Well?

REBECCA. You told me not to tell you.

RICHARD. Something must be done before it's too late! Where is he? I thought he was expecting you.

REBECCA. He promised he'd be here.

RICHARD. Promises are meant to be broken – that was

always your father's philosophy. At least it used to be. God, I miss that man!…We used to think alike – the Tiger Shark of Industry! The Wolf of Wall Street! That man was a saint!

REBECCA. It's not as bad as it seems. *(doubtfully)* Is it?

RICHARD. Surely even you can see your father desperately needs help. I mean – he doesn't even have a phone! We have to come traipsing over here every time we want to talk to him! And tell me – **why** is it he doesn't have a phone?

REBECCA. *(reluctantly)* He didn't like the way the ringing looked.

RICHARD. He didn't like the way the ringing looked.

REBECCA. Yes – all those pointed, sharp edges in red and yellow are very irritating to –

RICHARD. Will you listen to yourself! He **sees** things, Rebecca! Floating in the air! Things normal people don't see.

REBECCA. *(defensively)* He doesn't see **things**, Richard.

(**RICHARD** *eyes her doubtfully.*)

(reluctantly) He sees sounds.

RICHARD. Oh, excuse me – he sees sounds. That's so much more reassuring. Whenever the telephone rings, it's those "pointed, sharp edges in red and yellow," and the barking Pekinese in 1B is "gray smoke," and your name, what is it again he sees when he hears your name?

REBECCA. A blue swirl with a touch of pink, like a big lollipop. I used to like lollipops.

RICHARD. Rebecca! Need I remind you you're no longer a child? And corporate giants don't see sounds. Do you want to know why? Because if they did, that would mean they're **crazy**. *(suddenly anxious)* You don't think he's at Jersey's Market again? Didn't they ban him after the incident with that woman and her melons?

REBECCA. He only asked that woman to **say** the word "melons."

RICHARD. *(sarcastically)* Yes – he told her the sound of her melons formed such lovely squishy things. Christ! You can't imagine the anguish! The humiliation!

REBECCA. I suppose she was quite upset.

RICHARD. Not the woman! Me! What would have happened if she'd found out your father was Roger Cabot? She wouldn't have been saying, "melons, melons, melons," she would have been saying, "millions, millions, millions"! Can you imagine what the headlines would have read? "Fortune 500 Prez's Fruitful Fantasy" plastered over a picture of that woman and her – melons!

REBECCA. He can't help what he sees.

RICHARD. For God's sake, Rebecca! It's not just what he sees; it's what he's **become**! Spending more and more of his time and money on this **addiction** of his while I've been downgraded to little more than a middleman at the company!

REBECCA. But Richard –

RICHARD. Now, Rebecca! If you're to be my wife, we have to be united on this. We have to face the truth head on. No more denials. No more pretending. You haven't told anyone, have you?

REBECCA. You mean that Dad's become an artist?

RICHARD. Don't say it out loud for God's sake! It's unspeakable! If the stockholders got wind of this it would ruin everything!…And what *is* that disgusting smell?

REBECCA. Turpentine.

RICHARD. *(crossing to the curtained French doors and throwing open the curtains, then opening doors to air the loft)* He's probably been drinking it! *(spotting the rock formations on the patio)* Are those **boulders** out there?

REBECCA. It's Dad's Zen rock garden.

RICHARD. A Zen rock garden?! It's worse than I feared! All this tranquillity and spiritual crap is just further evidence of your father's corroding mental condition! *(spotting **ROGER** on the patio, speaking in shock)* Good God!

REBECCA. What is it?

RICHARD. Your father's out on the patio – *naked*!

REBECCA. Not again!

RICHARD. Again?!

REBECCA. I didn't want to tell you – but it's become a problem with the neighbors across the courtyard. *(calling out to the patio)* Dad! Will you please put your clothes on and get in here!

RICHARD. Oh – he's hopeless! Just look at him!

(REBECCA makes a move to look.)

No! Don't look!

(He gets caught up momentarily in the hanging crystals.)

What – what – ?! Damn it! What are these – these dangling things?

REBECCA. Crystals, Dear. Recently Dad's started to believe in the power of crystals.

RICHARD. My God! And he used to believe in the power of money. *(looking again on the patio, shocked)* Rebecca! What on earth is your father putting on?

REBECCA. Oh – that's all he wears these days. They're yugatas. *(pronounced "yew-GA-ta")* Traditional Japanese robes.

RICHARD. Well, a real man shouldn't show his yugatas in public!

(ROGER appears in the French doorway, watching RICH-ARD who mumbles to himself while trying to sit on the chair-like sculpture, contorting himself in various positions trying to get comfortable until he ends up in a very uncomfortable-looking position.)

Crystals…Zen rock garden…He doesn't even have a decent chair to sit on!

ROGER. *(entering fully, crossing to RICHARD)* Do you mind? You're sitting on my sculpture.

(RICHARD leaps up, and ROGER whisks off the large cloth, revealing the sculpture.)

I call it "Millennium's End: Seating for None." *(brightly as he crosses to* **REBECCA***)* Sweetheart – what a pleasure!

(He kisses her, then speaking unhappily.)

You didn't say you were bringing – Dick – with you.

RICHARD. It's Richard, Sir. *(to* **REBECCA***)* See? He can't even remember my name.

ROGER. You forget – you've worked for me for ten years. Believe me – you're a Dick.

REBECCA. Well, it was Richard's idea to come, Dad. We're worried about you.

ROGER. *(sarcastically, to* **RICHARD***)* How sweet. But as you can see – there's nothing to worry about. Look – I'm expecting someone.

RICHARD. One of those models, I suppose.

ROGER. As a matter of fact – yes.

RICHARD. If you don't mind my saying so, Sir –

ROGER. Is there any chance in hell you'll stop if I do mind?

RICHARD. Isn't it a bit unseemly at your age – you and these models as young as your own daughter? We all know painting isn't the only thing that goes on here.

ROGER. And your point would be – ?

RICHARD. In this day and age shouldn't you be more discerning about – well – you know – about –

ROGER. Where I dip my paintbrush?

RICHARD. Precisely.

ROGER. Why, Richard – I never knew you cared so much about my paintbrush.

RICHARD. Of course I do – I mean – I don't! I never think of your paintbrush! Ever!

ROGER. *(ushering* **RICHARD** *and* **REBECCA** *toward the downstage right door)* That's reassuring. Well, thanks for the fatherly advice. That model should be here any minute. So nice to see you. Come again. Any time. When hell freezes over.

REBECCA. Dad, Richard wants to talk to you about something else. We've come all this way.

ROGER. Oh – very well. She's late anyway. I'll just go down to 1B and call the art studio to see what's keeping her. Then we can have our little chat.

(He crosses to leave, then pauses.)

Oh, by the way – I think you both should know something – I'm selling the company.

RICHARD. Selling the company?

ROGER. I was thinking of giving some of the money to Green Peace.

RICHARD. *(horrified)* Green Peace?! But you always despised tree huggers and whale lovers. How can you give them your money?

ROGER. I like the way the name looks – Green Peace – such a soothing wave of aqua...

REBECCA. But Dad, the company's been in our family for generations.

ROGER. Don't worry, Rebecca – I've set aside a bit for you. Although you might have to supplement it with a job.

RICHARD. Supplement?! – with a – *job*?!

REBECCA. I don't care about the money, Dad. You've already given me everything I ever wanted.

ROGER. Sometimes I worry that's all I gave you – things. I wonder if I wasn't there enough for you when you were growing up.

REBECCA. I have only fond memories of growing up. Of the cook baking cookies in the kitchen, the au pair driving me to ballet and soccer, the chauffeur teaching me to drive, and of you –

ROGER. Yes? What are your fond memories of me?

REBECCA. Why – I – I – there must be something – oh, yes! I remember seeing the back of your Mercedes as the chauffeur drove you off each morning to the City.

ROGER. Not much of a father, was I? I want to make up for that.

RICHARD. You could hardly have neglected your responsibility to the company just for your daughter. You've devoted your entire life to that place.

ROGER. Correction. My entire past life.

(**ROGER** *exits downstage right.*)

REBECCA. I never had to have a job before! Dad may not have been there for my dance recitals or the holidays or my birthdays or my graduations, but he did every possible material thing for me.

RICHARD. Yes, he was a wonderful father.

REBECCA. I never had to work for anything. All I was ever good at was being seen and not heard.

RICHARD. Well, just keep doing that, Dear.

REBECCA. Don't you see? He took care of my life for me! I don't know how to do anything on my own!…Although I did graduate from college.

RICHARD. In *photography*, Rebecca. A nice hobby, perhaps, but not much good on a resume.

REBECCA. Oh, Richard – you're right! If Dad loses his mind, what will I do?

RICHARD. Does everything have to be about you? What will *I* do? He was grooming me to be president! Now I'll be downsized, just like everybody else!

REBECCA. We'll still have each other. We can draw strength from that.

RICHARD. That's very nice, Rebecca. But what's that without your father's wealth? I mean, your father's *health*! You know the money means nothing to me. It's just green paper, filthy lucre – that can buy practically anything I could possibly want – except happiness, of course, darling. Only you can bring me happiness.

REBECCA. I wouldn't blame you if you wanted to – to end it.

RICHARD. End it?

REBECCA. Call off our engagement. Under the circumstances. I might end up like my Dad, you know. It might be hereditary.

RICHARD. Believe me – you're nothing like your father, Rebecca.

REBECCA. Oh, Richard. That's the nicest thing anyone's ever said to me. Then you do find me attractive, don't you? You do love me?

RICHARD. You have all the qualities I value in a woman, Rebecca. You're quiet. Unassuming. You need someone to protect you. To handle all those bothersome financial details. I want to be that someone.

REBECCA. And to be the father of our children?

RICHARD. Children? You mean those tiny people with high-pitched voices?

REBECCA. I thought maybe we could start – well – you know – practicing.

RICHARD. Practicing? All right. How about right now?

REBECCA. Right now? Here?

RICHARD. I have to warn you, I think I'm going to be pretty good at this.

REBECCA. Oh, I hope so.

RICHARD. Shall I go first?

REBECCA. Don't people usually do it together?

RICHARD. Well, of course I'll need your help. I'd feel silly doing it alone. Now just stand right there.

(**REBECCA** *stands expectantly as* **RICHARD** *holds her by the shoulders.*)

Are you ready?

REBECCA. Ready.

RICHARD. Stand up straight!

(**REBECCA** *stands up straight.*)

Let me see your hands!

(**REBECCA** *holds out her hands.*)

Filthy! Filthy! Filthy! Go wash those hands immediately or I'll send you to your room! And don't bother me – I'm working!...Hey, this is fun!

REBECCA. I meant practicing what people do to *have* children.

RICHARD. *(shocked)* Rebecca! I'm beginning to wonder if the apple doesn't fall far from the tree after all! You do say the most appalling things sometimes.

REBECCA. Are you nervous because – well, because you may not think you're experienced enough? Because let me assure you, I wouldn't know the difference.

RICHARD. My sexual inexperience has nothing to do with it! I mean – I *am* experienced! *Plenty* experienced!

REBECCA. Just not with me.

RICHARD. Of course not with you! What a dreadful thought!...I like to think of our love as pure and chaste. *(indicating the painting, which both of them stare at)* Not tawdry and – like this – this revolting thing!

REBECCA. It's just a nude woman.

RICHARD. A *purple* nude woman. With amber circles flying around her head and those – those yellowish-green swirls all over her – her –

REBECCA. Her breast.

RICHARD. I know what it is. And – what is that – that pale, flaccid, snaky thing lying on her belly? Oh my God! Avert your eyes, Rebecca!

REBECCA. It's only a swan, Richard. See? That snaky part is it's neck. Although I suppose symbolically it *is* a –

RICHARD. Rebecca! Please! I have a problem with this.

REBECCA. Yes, I can see that.

RICHARD. We need to get all of this settled before we get married. I think it's time we both admit that professional help is in order. Do you agree?

REBECCA. Completely.

RICHARD. Good. That's why I've asked Dr. Stewart to meet us here this afternoon. He's a – he's a – psychiatrist.

REBECCA. That's wonderful, Richard – that you'd be willing to consult a psychiatrist about this problem. But surely he's not going to analyze you here?

RICHARD. Not a psychiatrist for *me*! For your *father*!

REBECCA. I don't think Dad's the one who needs a sex therapist, Richard.

RICHARD. A *sex* therapist?!

REBECCA. I can be very patient, Darling. I know a marriage isn't all about sex. At least, that's what Mom always said.

RICHARD. I'd rather not think about your mother and sex at the same time, if you don't mind. And Dr. Stewart isn't a sex therapist! He's just a regular – psychiatrist – for your *father*!

REBECCA. *(suspiciously)* Not the kind who makes you curl up in a fetal position and scream, I hope?

RICHARD. You know I don't do that anymore!

REBECCA. And remember the last psychiatrist you referred Dad to?

RICHARD. It's not my fault that didn't work out. How could I have known Dr. Pinkerton was into thumb sucking?

*(**RICHARD** whines, shaking his head and hands as if they were made of rubber.)*

REBECCA. Richard? Are you all right?

RICHARD. Damn it, Rebecca! I'm releasing tension. *(Again* **RICHARD** *whines, shaking his head and hands.)* It's Whining Therapy. I didn't get to whine enough when I was a child. *(regaining his composure)* Jason Stewart is different. We were fraternity brothers. If you really want to help your father, just go along with whatever I say.

ROGER. *(entering)* The studio doesn't know where the model is. They're going to try and send someone else…. Now what was it you so desperately needed to speak to me about?

REBECCA. Well, I'll just come right out and say it, Dad. Richard has made arrangements to have –

*(As **REBECCA** begins to speak **RICHARD** positions himself behind **ROGER** and signals to **REBECCA** that she is not to reveal that a psychiatrist is expected. **ROGER** suddenly*

looks behind him and **RICHARD** *instantly transforms his motions into a mime of T'ai Chi.)*

RICHARD. T'ai Chi lessons.

ROGER. *(suspiciously)* Yes – that is a bit hard to take.

RICHARD. Well, ever since you took it up, I've been inspired. Searching for spiritual awareness in this dog-eat-dog world.

ROGER. You usually have to have a soul for that, Dick.

RICHARD. *(ceasing the T'ai Chi movements)* It's **Richard** – *Sir.* Actually, the reason we're here is to arrange a meeting with you and – and – my brother.

REBECCA. I thought you were an only child?

RICHARD. *(pointedly)* Don't you remember my **brother**? The one who will be here **any minute**?

REBECCA. Oh yes! Your **brother**. He should be here **any minute**.

ROGER. *(to himself)* And they think **I'm** losing my mind. *(to* **RICHARD***)* And does this previously unknown brother have a name?

REBECCA. *(beginning to say "Doctor")* It's Doc –

RICHARD. *(interrupting quickly, with affirmation)* Da! That's his name.

ROGER. Da?

RICHARD. It's an old family nickname.

ROGER. Which is short for –?

RICHARD. Da – Da – Dante.

ROGER. *(reacting as if seeing shapes in front of him as he says the name)* Da – Da – Dante …

　　　(to **RICHARD***)*

Is he anything like you?

RICHARD. Not really.

ROGER. Then I'd love to meet him. Just what does Dante do?

REBECCA. He's a psychia –

RICHARD. Cyclist! – He's a cyclist.

ROGER. A cyclist?

REBECCA.   RICHARD.

Bicyclist.   Motorcyclist.

RICHARD. *Motorcyclist*, Rebecca. I ought to know my own brother.

ROGER. I meant – what does Dante do for a living?

RICHARD. Dante?

ROGER. Your brother?

RICHARD. Oh – my **brother** Dante – well he – *(glancing around at the paintings)* He – he owns an art gallery.

REBECCA. An art gallery?

RICHARD. Yes – an art gallery, Rebecca. You know you told Dante about your father's paintings, and he's quite excited about seeing them. *(to* **ROGER***, pointedly)* He has **lots** of questions to ask you. Isn't that right, Rebecca?

REBECCA. Oh, yes. *Lots* of questions.

RICHARD. Maybe you could have a one-man show if you answer those questions.

ROGER. I thought you didn't approve of my paintings.

RICHARD. What? No! I love them, Sir!

ROGER. You do? Maybe you're not so bad after all. *(indicating the painting)* Tell me what you love about this one.

RICHARD. This one? *(examining the painting, trying to hide his distaste)* Well, for one thing, it's – so – very – very – very – purple. I don't think I've ever seen a naked woman so very purple before.

ROGER. It's called *Leda in Purple*. Picasso had his Blue Period. I have my purple. Anything else you like about it?

RICHARD. Um…It's big. But not too big. It's just right. Would fit in perfectly just about anywhere.

ROGER. How about your apartment?

RICHARD. *My* apartment?

ROGER. Yes – I'm giving it to you.

RICHARD. You can't! I mean – I can't accept such a generous gift.

ROGER. Why not?

RICHARD. It's too awful – some. Awesome. So awesome, it makes me want to cry. I just couldn't take this from you.

ROGER. Don't you intend to marry my daughter ?

RICHARD. Well – um – yes.

ROGER. Well, then, I expect I'll be offering you all sorts of gifts. Are you telling me you're going to refuse them all?

RICHARD. (to **REBECCA**, *as he quickly starts to move the painting)* Well don't just stand there, Darling. Help me take this to the car.

(**REBECCA** and **RICHARD** *cross to the apartment door, carrying the painting.)*

ROGER. You'll have to take the stairs. It won't fit in the elevator.

RICHARD. Great.

(**RICHARD** and **REBECCA** *exit carrying the painting.)*

ROGER. *(calling after them)* Enjoy! *(to himself)* Now if only that model would show.

(The intercom buzzer BUZZES.)

(seeing the sound of the buzzer) Nasty yellow slash!

(**ROGER** *crosses to the intercom. Pushing the intercom buzzer and speaking into the intercom:)*

Yes?

ABIGAIL. *(over intercom)* Is this Roger Cabot's place?

ROGER. *(speaking into intercom)* It's about time! The light's fading. Come on up. The door's open. I'll be setting everything up. And take your clothes off as soon as you get here. I want to get right to it.

(**ROGER** *crosses to the table next to the easel and selects a few paint brushes. He exits onto the patio, crossing to an* *unseen portion of the patio and returning just outside the French doors with a large easel. Periodically throughout the scene he exits to the unseen part of the patio, returning alternately with a stool, a small table with paint supplies, and finally a large canvas. The audience sees these movements.* **ABIGAIL** *and* **JASON** *do not immediately see him.)*

*(***DOCTOR JASON STEWART*** knocks on the opened door, then he and* **ABIGAIL EVANS**, *who is carrying a file folder and a note pad and pen, enter fully.)*

(He is attractive, sincere, and clumsy around **REBECCA**. *He is dressed in an expensive suit, dress shirt and tie.)*

(She is attractive with a good figure and is sarcastic, but a bit of a romantic underneath. She is dressed in tasteful clothes which show off her figure.)

JASON. Hello? Richard? Anyone here? Strange. *Someone* told us to come up.

ABIGAIL. And take off our clothes so we could get right to it, don't forget.

JASON. Well, we're not going to do that.

ABIGAIL. *(sarcastically)* Uncanny – have you always been so perceptive?

JASON. Can we do without your smart remarks for once?

ABIGAIL. Probably not.

JASON. Just take notes, Abigail. That's what I'm paying you for.

ABIGAIL. In case you've forgotten, I'm not your secretary. I'm a free-lance writer, and you're paying me to ghostwrite your book – *Neuro-Laser Brain Surgery for the Terminally Wealthy.* Believe me, I deserve every dime.

JASON. So this isn't the highfalutin subject matter you usually write about for the *National Scuttlebutt.* What was that last probing piece of yours? That exemplar of veracity in journalism?

ABIGAIL. Ah, yes – "Cattle Mutilations Linked to Senator's Sex Romp." I have the photos if you want to see them.

JASON. No thanks. (*checking his watch*) Richard's late.

ABIGAIL. (*crossing to and looking inside the upstage left door*) That must have been Roger Cabot who buzzed us up. I wonder where he's hiding.

JASON. Better not find him until Richard gets here. He's asked me to evaluate the man. Informally, of course. He thought my latest surgical technique might help. (*musing*) You know, until that reception last month I hadn't seen Richard Borman since our Tri Delta Phi days….He had it all – looks, ability, ambition.

ABIGAIL. It sounds like you still envy him.

JASON. Don't be ridiculous, Abigail. I'm a neurosurgeon. I don't envy anyone.

(**ROGER** *struggles to put the canvas on the easel, speaking to the model he thinks has arrived*)

ROGER. Are you there?

ABIGAIL. (*to* **JASON**) Are we here?

(**JASON** *nods and* **ABIGAIL** *responds to* **ROGER**.)

Yes!

ROGER. Well, get your clothes off and come on out here. I'll have this up in a minute.

JASON. It's more serious than I thought! Where the hell is Richard?

(**ROGER** *turns on a radio.*)

(*MUSIC is heard from the patio.*)

(**ABIGAIL** *and* **JASON** *cross to look through the French doors at* **ROGER**, *who is "seeing" the music and verbally and physically responding to what he sees.*)

ABIGAIL. (*to* **JASON**) Who is he talking to?

JASON. According to Richard he hallucinates and has been exhibiting some bizarre and paranoid behavior.

ABIGAIL. Oh – speaking of bizarre and paranoid – your fiancee called.

JASON. Avis called? What did she say?

ABIGAIL. Ms. Avis Harpinger said to tell you that your

Honey Bunny still has some court briefs to work on, so she's changed the reservations to Chez Louis for eight o'clock.

JASON. Chez Louis? Again? We ate there on Wednesday and last Friday.

ABIGAIL. I can't understand why you don't just agree on another restaurant.

JASON. She's a lawyer, Abigail. It's her job to be disagreeable.

ABIGAIL. Well she must be a very **good** lawyer, then. Oh – by the way, she wanted you to phone her immediately.

JASON. *(suddenly anxious)* **When** did she say to phone her immediately?

ABIGAIL. Oh – about an hour ago.

JASON. An hour ago! Why didn't you tell me before now?

(Frantically, he begins to search for a phone.)

ROGER. *(calling to* **ABIGAIL,** *referring to the sunlight)* Hurry up! It's fading!

JASON. Where the devil is the phone?

ABIGAIL. There doesn't seem to be one.

JASON. At least Avis mustn't be too angry with me. She hasn't beeped me yet.

ABIGAIL. *(pulling his beeper from her pocket)* I was wondering what that buzzing sensation was.

JASON. *(angrily grabbing the beeper from her, then crossing quickly to the downstage right door)* I'm going to the car and use my cell phone. Wait here in case Richard finally decides to show up.

(He exits just as **ROGER** *crosses to the French doors.)*

(The MUSIC ceases.)

ROGER. *(eyeing* **ABIGAIL** *as he enters fully)* Such voluptuous curves – like a Boticcelli.

ABIGAIL. You must be Roger Cabot.

ROGER. Just call me Roger. I never liked the look of my last name – grey squares with puce stripes. *(walking around* *her, appraising what he sees)* You're not at all like the skinny ones I've had lately. More than a bit older, too.

ABIGAIL. Thanks for noticing.

ROGER. I meant it as a compliment. What's your name?

ABIGAIL. Abigail.

ROGER. *(gazing at the colored shapes her name makes)* Abigail – like warm caramel half moons melting on my tongue…I've been waiting for you.

ABIGAIL. All your life, I suppose?

ROGER. No – out on the patio. Now enough chit-chat. Go ahead and take off your clothes. I'm anxious to begin!

ABIGAIL. *(amused)* Well, that's the most direct offer I've had in a long time.

ROGER. By the way – you're not a complainer, are you?

ABIGAIL. Not usually.

ROGER. Good. If I have to hear one more time about how tiring it is to hold the same position for hours and how long it takes me to finish –

ABIGAIL. Did you say *hours*?

ROGER. Well, of course the whole process takes days, but I give them breaks. Fifteen minutes off, 45 minutes on.

ABIGAIL. *Days*?

ROGER. Once it took an entire month. And I still wasn't satisfied in the end. I hope you'll be able to hold still for long stretches. The last girl was quiet, but kept moving about. It makes things a bit difficult, considering I'm doing all the work.

ABIGAIL. You mean she didn't moan or anything?

ROGER. Thank God, no. I told her to just lie there and think of England…You still have your clothes on.

ABIGAIL. I'm sorry to disappoint you, but I usually don't get naked with strange men.

ROGER. Aren't you from the modeling agency?

ABIGAIL. Modeling agency? Oh…No. I'm meeting Richard Borman.

ROGER. Richard? Oh. I'm afraid he'll be back. *(looking at* *her with sudden confusion)* You're – you're not Richard's – **brother**, are you?

ABIGAIL. Do I **look** like someone's brother?

ROGER. You never know these days. But no – you look quite lovely, really. It's just that I was expecting a model and Richard's brother – and you don't seem to be either.

ABIGAIL. Oh! Richard's **brother**. Tri Delta Phi and all that.

ROGER. I thought it was Dante?

ABIGAIL. Could be. I can never keep those Greek names straight. He should be back in a minute.

ROGER. *(eagerly)* He's been here already? Did he see everything?

ABIGAIL. I'm pretty sure he saw enough.

ROGER. Tell me – what did he think? Be honest.

ABIGAIL. Well – he thinks he might be able to help you.

ROGER. Wonderful! Your words have inspired me! Your name inspires me! You inspire me!

ABIGAIL. *I* inspire you? But we've just met.

ROGER. Sometimes that's all it takes – just meeting….You know, I was more than a bit surprised when Richard arranged this little session. In fact, I had my doubts this Dante brother even existed. Richard's become like the Shark in so many ways.

ABIGAIL. Sounds like you don't like him much.

ROGER. Actually there was a time when I considered Richard like a son. He and I agreed on practically everything. But now I'm getting rid of my attachment to material things. Simplifying my life. It's not something Richard understands.

ABIGAIL. Material things are what most people think they want out of life. But from what I've seen, actually having them doesn't seem to make anyone happier.

ROGER. No. It doesn't…What about you? You don't seem to be like most people.

ABIGAIL. I have what I want – a writing career that's paid for a nice condo and given me the freedom to go wherever I choose.

ROGER. That's not what you want.

ABIGAIL. So why don't you tell me what I want if you know so much.

ROGER. What is it your heart has always yearned for? Quick! Say the first thing that pops into your head.

ABIGAIL. To write a novel that has absolutely nothing to do with celebrities or politicians or neurosurgeons… and…

ROGER. And? …Anything to do with you being all alone in that condo of yours?

ABIGAIL. And I think I'll keep that second thought to myself.

ROGER. You should chuck it all and write that novel.

ABIGAIL. You make it sound so simple.

ROGER. Trust me. It is.

ABIGAIL. You are strange.

ROGER. But somehow appealing?

ABIGAIL. Perhaps.

ROGER. There's some life to you. Experience behind those lovely eyes. It would be a shame for that to go to waste. Abigail – warm caramel half moons melting on my tongue…When he gets back tell him I've gone out to paint in the last rays of sunset.

(*He moves to depart through the French doors, then pauses.*)

Too bad you're not my model. It would be so nice to see you unfettered by all those clothes.

(*He exits through the French doors.*)

JASON. (*entering, carrying a cell phone*) Well, I hope you're happy. Avis left three angry messages on my voice mail. And she's not even answering her pager.

ABIGAIL. You can thank me later.

JASON. You don't like Avis. Admit it.

ABIGAIL. That's not true. I detest Avis.

JASON. Really, Abigail! I don't know what you can possibly have against her.

ABIGAIL. I was wondering the same thing about you.

JASON. You couldn't have formed a fair opinion. The first time you met her was only a month ago.

ABIGAIL. Yes – at that reception. She mistook me for a coat rack, as I recall.

JASON. I see Richard hasn't shown up.

ABIGAIL. Not yet. But I had an interesting conversation with our friend on the patio.

JASON. What did he say?

ABIGAIL. Let's just say if you look up the word "eccentric" – Roger Cabot is the first definition. But he knows all about you and seems very eager for you to do your thing.

JASON. I still have to see if he's an appropriate candidate. I don't just "do my thing" on anybody.

ABIGAIL. No, you've been very selective about whom you do your thing on – like at those medical conferences.

JASON. Just what are you insinuating?

ABIGAIL. You come home from your third conference this month looking like a little boy who's spent all night alone in a candy shop. It doesn't take a neurosurgeon to figure it out.

JASON. I always find medical talk stimulating.

ABIGAIL. You're being stimulated by something, all right. Unfortunately, Avis thinks it's me.

JASON. Avis thinks I'm sleeping with you? What a ridiculous idea!

ABIGAIL. Well, thanks a lot.

JASON. That's not what I meant. Avis is a beautiful, highly successful lawyer who was very interested that I was a neurosurgeon. She was determined to have me. Said we'd make the perfect couple. What more could I want?

ABIGAIL. Some passion, maybe? There's obviously no sexual

spark between you two.

JASON. No sexual spark?! We're sparking all the time!

ABIGAIL. Yeah – like two limp noodles rubbing together.

JASON. Like fireworks we spark! We spark all over the place! Spark! Spark! Spark! We can't stop sparking! Not that it's any of your business.

ABIGAIL. I may have only known you a few months, Jason, but I've seen what you're like when you're really attracted to someone.

JASON. And just what am I like?

ABIGAIL. Remember that woman at the reception last month?

(**JASON** *gets a far-away look of love in his eyes and accidentally knocks over the small table next to the easel, upsetting the brushes and tubes of paint onto the floor. He quickly begins picking up the mess.*)

That's how you get. Clumsy. Don't get me wrong – it's rather sweet, really.

JASON. I am a neurosurgeon, Abigail. I am not clumsy.

(*He bungles picking up the brushes.*)

That doesn't count!

(*He hastily replaces the brushes and paint tubes.*)

ABIGAIL. You're never clumsy around Avis.

JASON. For your information, I couldn't love Avis less – I mean – more! I couldn't love her more! I don't even know that woman's name, and I haven't seen her since. And I don't need your Dear Abby advice, thank you very much! I can handle my sex life on my own.

ABIGAIL. With Avis for a girlfriend, I'm sure you do that all the time.

JASON. (*grabbing the folder from her*) Oh – just give me the folder...Richard's number is in here somewhere...

(*As* **JASON** *begins to search through the folder,* **REBECCA** *and* **RICHARD** *enter.* **RICHARD** *clears his throat to get* **JASON** *and* **ABIGAIL**'s *attention.*)

(Spotting **REBECCA** *immediately, speaking to himself.)*

My God! It's her!

(The cell phone and the contents of the folder spill to the floor. He kneels and begins picking up the papers.)

RICHARD. Jason?

JASON. Richard – uh – I – just a minute.

ABIGAIL. *(kneeling beside him, picking up the cell phone)* Let me help.

JASON. *(hastily stuffing the papers into the folder, speaking with a hiss to* **ABIGAIL***)* These hands have worked on delicate parts of the body. I think I can manage a few papers.

(Some of the papers fall out again, and **JASON** *must redo his efforts.)*

ABIGAIL. *(quietly, so that* **RICHARD** *and* **REBECCA** *can not hear)* Isn't that the woman from the reception?

JASON. *(quietly, so that* **RICHARD** *and* **REBECCA** *can not hear)* Yes! It's her! God, she's so lovely!

(Finally finished with the folder, he leaps up, speaking so that all can hear.)

There!...Richard –

RICHARD & JASON *(shaking hands in a ritualistic manner while reciting together)* Tri-Delta-Phi! Never say die! Blood's not thicker than this school tie! If one doth break this sacred bond – the other shall see the great beyond! Brrrrrooooothers Forever! Sis! Boom! Ba!

ABIGAIL. *(to* **REBECCA***)* Male bonding.

RICHARD. Thank you for coming, Jason. I guess you've already met Roger.

JASON. As a matter of fact – no. He's out on the patio. I thought it best to wait until you got here.

RICHARD. Good. We need to get our story straight.

JASON. This is Abigail Evans. She'll just be taking a few notes.

RICHARD. Well, all right. But Roger can't know right away who you really are.

JASON. I don't know, Richard…

REBECCA. Please? He's very resistant to any kind of treatment.

RICHARD. Jason – this is my fiancee – Rebecca Cabot – Roger's daughter.

JASON. You're engaged?

REBECCA. It only happened recently.

ABIGAIL. He who hesitates …

JASON. Thank you, Abigail.

REBECCA. It's so nice to see you again.

JASON. *(holding out his hand to shake* **REBECCA***'s)* And you, Miss Cabot –

(He drops the folder and papers. He quickly kneels to pick them up.)

REBECCA. *(kneeling beside him)* Let me help you.

JASON. *(sneaking longing looks at her)* How kind of you.

(As she hands some papers to **JASON***, their fingers touch and they gaze into each other's eyes.)*

ABIGAIL. *(in* **JASON***'s ear)* Don't you want to tell her how your hands work on delicate parts of the body?

JASON. I said thank you, Abigail.

RICHARD. You two have already met?

REBECCA. At that reception you took me to last month. Dr. Stewart and I had a very stimulating conversation about photography and the environment and never even found out each other's names.

RICHARD. Fascinating.

JASON. I won't let on who I am for the time being, if that's what you want, Miss Cabot.

REBECCA. Thank you. And please – call me Rebecca.

JASON. Rebecca…I always liked the name Rebecca.

REBECCA. Oh – well, thank you Dr. Stewart.

JASON. Please – just call me Jason.

REBECCA. Jason…I always liked the name Jason.

ABIGAIL. Is this synchronicity or what?

RICHARD. Yes, yes. Rebecca and Jason are perfectly nice names. Now that we've established that, can we please just get on with it?

JASON. Of course. *(to* **REBECCA***)* But before we call your father in, why don't you tell me everything?

RICHARD. I've already told you everything you need to know.

JASON. I want to hear from Rebecca's own lips.

REBECCA. Oh – thank you, Jason. Why don't we all sit down.

(They all search for some place to sit.)

RICHARD. For God's sake! There's no place to sit!

*(***ABIGAIL*** immediately settles herself on the table/bench with her notepad. ***REBECCA*** sits on a throw pillow near the sculpture chair. ***JASON*** tries unsuccessfully to sit in the uncomfortable sculpture chair, ending up posed in an awkward position in the chair which he pretends is comfortable. ***RICHARD*** remains standing.)*

REBECCA. I'm not sure where to begin. Dad seems to be – a completely different person than the Dad I knew.

JASON. *(comforting her)* It's all right. You can tell me. That's why I'm here.

RICHARD. It really is too horrible.

JASON. I'm a doctor. I'm used to horrible things.

ABIGAIL. You should see Ms. Harpinger.

REBECCA. Who's Ms. Harpinger?

JASON. *(giving* **ABIGAIL** *a piercing look)* No one.

ABIGAIL. I'll make a note of that.

JASON. Go ahead, Rebecca.

REBECCA. It started after my mother's death last year – this change in Dad's behavior. So naturally I thought – I thought at first it was all because of grief.

RICHARD. The real nightmare began when Mr. Cabot took those Life Drawing classes and started inviting young women here at all hours – to pose in the nude!

ABIGAIL. It's amazing what grief will do.

RICHARD. (drawing **JASON** over to where the paintings are stored and pulling out a painting) They say a picture's worth a thousand words. Well – **this** should say it all.

(**JASON** is quite taken with what he sees. **RICHARD** points to a portion of the painting.)

Look at this – this –

JASON. Breast…

RICHARD. Not that! The grey smoke! That's the barking from 1B. And this –

(pointing to another section)

– this orange, squishy thing is the sound of melons.

JASON. And what's that thing that looks like a peacock?

RICHARD. It **is** a peacock….The point is, Roger Cabot used to be an icon in the business world! Now all he paints are these gargantuan canvases with nude purple women and birds and these things he sees.

JASON. I'm afraid I've come across this before. Drastic personality change, lack of inhibition.

RICHARD. That's the understatement of the year! We used to call him The Shark at the office. But now – well, you can't believe what comes out of his mouth.

JASON. He swears uncontrollably at people, does he?

RICHARD. (sadly) Not like he used to.

JASON. (confused) Well, then, does he humiliate people, make them feel small and helpless?

RICHARD. (wistfully) Those days are gone. God, I idolized that man!

JASON. What kind of outrageous things **does** he say?

RICHARD. He tells the truth! In front of everyone!…Just the other day he told us he'd had great sex the night before with one of his models. Right there on the floor, rolling around in all that paint. Can you imagine?

JASON. Give me a moment.

RICHARD. Snap out of it, man! You don't tell your daughter about your sex life!

REBECCA. In all fairness to Dad, it wasn't just sex. When he was done, he'd discovered he'd created a new painting. He calls it Horizontal Mambo.

RICHARD. Rebecca! You are forever defending that man! It was nothing more than sex! Depraved, loathsome, repulsive sex, sex, sex!

REBECCA. *(gazing at* **JASON***)* I'm sure he was only trying to make human contact.

*(***JASON*** *leans toward her.)*

RICHARD. Oh – he made contact all right.

REBECCA. *(She leans closer to* **JASON***.)* That is only natural, isn't it? – to make contact?

JASON. Yes…only natural…

*(***JASON*** *leans closer still and falls out of the chair.)*

RICHARD. *(indicating the painting)* Well if that doesn't indicate something's wrong with the man's brain, I don't know what does! Except perhaps those things he sees floating around! And if you can't comprehend that your father needs help, Rebecca, well then – I just don't know!

*(***RICHARD*** *storms away, exiting onto the patio.)*

JASON. I can see you're worried about your father, Rebecca. You seem to be a very caring, very sensitive, very beautiful woman.

REBECCA. I do?

JASON. Yes – you do. Don't worry – there could be many explanations for your father's behavior. But you know, I'm curious about something Richard just said – about your father seeing things floating around?

REBECCA. It started about six months after Mom died. Every sound he heard started to take shape in front of his eyes. The rumble of thunder was saffron splashes. The blare of a car horn – burnt orange smoke. Even a person's name formed into colored shapes – like a blue swirl with a touch of pink, like a lollipop.

ABIGAIL. Or warm caramel half moons melting on his tongue?

REBECCA. Does that mean he's going crazy?

JASON. He may be suffering from a rare condition called synesthesia. People with this condition can feel tastes, hear things they touch, or, as in your father's case, see sounds. It's caused by – well – in technical terms – by cross-wiring in the brain.

REBECCA. I see. Then there's no hope.

JASON. On the contrary. I believe he's an excellent candidate for a technique I've just developed.

REBECCA. Oh! If you could help I'd be so grateful, Dr. Stewart.

JASON. Jason, please.

REBECCA. Jason. Please.

(**JASON** *knocks over some paintings leaning against the wall.*)

ABIGAIL. Here we go again.

REBECCA. I feel I can place myself in your hands.

JASON. I'd love to have yourself in my hands.

(*They gaze into each other's eyes.*)

(*The cell phone RINGS.*)

ABIGAIL. (*answering the phone*) Hello? (*to* **JASON**) Jason. It's Honey Bunny.

JASON. (*taking the phone*) Thank you, Abigail. (*into the phone*) Hello? (*pause*) Of course I'm not avoiding you. (*glaring at* **ABIGAIL**) My beeper was indisposed. (*pause*) I'm sorry you have a migraine now.

(*Speaking quietly into the phone, trying to prevent* **REBECCA** *from hearing.*)

What? No, I haven't forgotten you're my – my fiancee.

REBECCA. (*with more disappointment, turning away from* **JASON**) Fiancee?

ABIGAIL. If it makes you want to puke now, just wait 'til you meet Honey Bunny.

JASON. Yes, I'm still at that address, but I might be here for awhile. *(pause, then speaking quickly)* No – don't come here! Avis? Avis?

(He hangs up.)

RICHARD. *(entering quickly from the patio)* Quick! He's coming! *(calling out to* **ROGER***)* Yes – Dante and his – his –*(He gestures at* **ABIGAIL.***)*

REBECCA. *(wistfully, to herself)* Fiancee…

RICHARD. *(calling out to* **ROGER***)* Fiancee! Dante and his fiancée are here!

JASON. Who's Dante?

RICHARD. Your name is Dante, you're not a doctor, you own an art gallery and you're considering Roger for a one-man show and you're an expert on motorcycles. And she –

(He thrusts **ABIGAIL** *into* **JASON***'s arms.)*

– is your fiancee. Just go with it.

ROGER. *(entering)* I was just in my Zen rock garden. I find it very relaxing. *(noticing the others are tense)* Maybe all of you should try it. *(moving to shake* **JASON***'s hand)* You must be Dante – large, soft black rectangles with smudges of orange. *(to* **ABIGAIL,** *disappointed)* And you're Dante's fiancee? Abigail – like warm caramel half moons melting on my tongue.

RICHARD. For God's sake! Will you please just answer Dante's questions – yes or no will do nicely.

ROGER. If you insist.

JASON. It's a pleasure to meet you. May I call you Roger?

ROGER. No.

JASON. Mr. Cabot, then?

ABIGAIL. He doesn't like the look of his last name.

JASON. Oh – well – would you prefer I call you something else?

ROGER. Yes.

JASON. *(When* **ROGER** *does not say what he wants to be called)* Would you like to tell us what that would be?

ROGER. No

RICHARD. Will you stop playing games! Do you think I'm a complete idiot?

ROGER. Yes.

RICHARD. That wasn't a question!

REBECCA. Dad! Will you behave!

ROGER. Probably not....I was just doing what Richard instructed.

JASON. We all just want you to be yourself, Roger. May I call you Roger?

ROGER. You can call me sweetheart if you're going to hang me in your gallery.

JASON. Oh, yes – my gallery.

(**JASON** *follows as* **ROGER** *crosses to the paintings leaning against the wall. As* **JASON** *flips through the canvases and comments,* **ROGER** *admires* **ABIGAIL**.)

Yes…. Very nice….

ROGER. (*still admiring* **ABIGAIL**) I was thinking the same thing myself.

JASON. (*continuing to examine the paintings*) Very naked.

ROGER. One can dream. You're a lucky man, Dante, to have such a lovely, intelligent woman like Abigail for your fiancee.

ABIGAIL. (*drawing her arm through Jason's*) Do you hear that, Jason? Don't you feel lucky?

JASON. (*sarcastically*) Yes, yes. She's a real treasure.

RICHARD. (*whispering in* **JASON**'s *ear*) Act the part, for God's sake.

ROGER. (*to* **ABIGAIL**) Maybe you'd consider posing for me? Especially since my model never showed up.

(**AVIS** *appears in the doorway. She has a definite presence – tall, slim, beautiful, self-centered and abrasive. She is dressed very professionally in a chic, black jacket and short, matching skirt.*)

JASON. (*drawing* **ABIGAIL** *to him*) I'm afraid that's out of the question. We're very attached to each other. I'm the only one she'll get naked with.

AVIS. *(entering fully)* Just as I suspected!

JASON. *(quickly pushing* ABIGAIL *away)* Avis!

AVIS. And just who should *I* get naked with?

ROGER. I believe that would be me. Quick! The light's fading!

JASON. *(to* AVIS*)* This isn't what it seems.

ROGER. Do you two know each other?

AVIS. I'll ask the questions! Now what's going on?

JASON. I can't tell you right now – Honey Bunny.

ROGER. We can answer questions later, Honey. May I call you "Honey"?

AVIS. You may not!

ROGER. Miss Bunny, it is, then. Quick! Go out on the patio and take off your clothes. I'll get rid of these people.

AVIS. What did you say?!

ROGER. *(speaking slowly)* Go out on the patio and take off your clothes. *(speaking normally)* I'll join you in a moment. You can look at my rocks.

AVIS. I can look at your what?!

ROGER. You can sit on them, too. If you're careful. They're delicately arranged. But I'm sure you'll find it relaxing. You seem very tense, and you should be relaxed before we start.

AVIS. Is this man a lunatic?

JASON, RICHARD, & REBECCA. *(together)* Yes.

AVIS. *(to* JASON*)* Did you or did you not just now admit you and Abigail were attached to each other?

ABIGAIL. *Very* attached, I believe were the exact words.

JASON. Thank you for that clarification, Abigail.

AVIS. Just answer my question!

JASON. I did say that, but –

AVIS. Yes or no will suffice.

JASON. But, Avis, I'm not guilty –

AVIS. That's what they all say! Now did you or did you not also admit you're the only person she'll get naked with?

JASON. It's just a figure of speech?

AVIS. Oh, please! I was wondering why you'd been going on so many of those out-of-town conferences lately. Now I know. You two have been having an affair, haven't you?

JASON. No!

ROGER. *(indicating* **JASON** *and* **ABIGAIL***)* But aren't you two engaged?

AVIS. *Engaged!*

ABIGAIL. As of just this afternoon. Isn't that right, Jason?

REBECCA. Maybe I can explain –

AVIS. I am not asking you a question! Although I reserve the right to do so at a later time.

(suddenly interested in **REBECCA***)*

You look familiar.

ABIGAIL. Reception. Strangers in the night. Exchanging glances.

JASON. *(to* **ABIGAIL***)* Wondering what were the chances you would shut up.

AVIS. Yes – I remember her now. I don't believe we've been formerly introduced.

JASON. Avis, this is Rebecca –

(He knocks over an empty can of turpentine, and as he tries to pick it up, accidentally kicks it.)

Cabot. Rebecca – this is –

*(***REBECCA*** and ***JASON*** look longing at each other.)*

AVIS. Avis Harpinger. *(Realizing* **REBECCA** *is her rival, turning from them, absently facing the painting against the wall, speaking sarcastically of the situation.)* Well, well, well – isn't this a pretty picture?

ROGER. I don't know that I'd call it pretty necessarily, but I'm glad you like it.

AVIS. *(waving her hand at the painting)* Not this tripe!

ROGER. Tripe?! First you're rude to my daughter, then you insult my painting! I don't care what you are to Dante. I want you to go! Go! Go! Go!

AVIS. Who the hell is Dante?

*(Everyone looks at **JASON**. **RICHARD** whines, shaking his head and hands.)*

JASON. *(raising his hand, speaking fearfully)* I am.

AVIS. *You* are? What is this, Jason? Some sicko double life? Because if it is – *(suddenly interested)* I want to hear all about it.

JASON. I'm not leading a double life! Abigail and I are not having an affair. We were just pretending to be engaged when you happened to walk in.

(after hesitating, then finally coming clean)

And I was just pretending to be Richard's brother Dante.

ROGER. You're not Dante?

REBECCA. Dad, there is no Dante.

ROGER. No Dante?…Then – there's no art gallery? No one-man show? Well –it seems you've all been having one over on me. Even my own daughter.

*(to **JASON**)*

But if you're not Dick's brother, then who the hell are you?

AVIS. This is *Doctor* Jason Stewart. *My* fiancee.

ROGER. *(to **JASON**)* My condolences.

(recognizing the name)

Doctor Jason Stewart? I've read about you in Scientific Discoveries. The question is – why are you here?

AVIS. I advise you not to answer any of this wacko's questions.

RICHARD. Dr. Stewart is only here to help you. And Rebecca and I agree – you do need help.

ROGER. Oh, Rebecca and you agree...Well, maybe you're right. Maybe I do need the doctor's help after all. Okay, Dr. Stewart – take off your clothes!

AVIS.	JASON.	REBECCA.	RICHARD.
What?!	Mr. Cabot!	Dad!	Revolting!

ROGER. Well, it's the only thing I need help with since that damn model never showed up!

REBECCA. Do you always have to be so embarrassing?

ROGER. Apparently I do....Now if you don't mind – I just want to be left alone to do what I want. Is there anything wrong with that?

REBECCA. No – there's nothing wrong with that! All you've done you're whole life is leave me alone and do what *you* want! Why should what I want mean anything to you now when it didn't mean anything when I was your little girl!

ROGER. And what is it you *do* want, Rebecca? *(indicating* **RICHARD***)* Other than to marry this calculating and conniving schemer.

RICHARD. Thank you, Sir. I always tried my best to emulate you.

REBECCA. I want you to be my old father again! At least I understood him!

ROGER. Don't you have anything you want to do on your own?

REBECCA. On my own? You mean by myself? Of course there is! I want to – I want to – Oh! I don't know what I want!

(She exits through the off-stage room door upstage left, slamming the door behind her. **ROGER** *winces at the sight of the sound of the slamming.)*

RICHARD. You're a despicable man! *(slapping* **ROGER** *on the back)* Almost like the old you.

*(***RICHARD** *exits after* **REBECCA***, slamming the door behind him.* **ROGER** *winces again at the sight of the sound of the slamming door.)*

JASON. *(to* **AVIS** *and* **ABIGAIL***)* Could you give us a moment?

AVIS. I'm sensing another migraine, Jason.

ABIGAIL. We'll just take a walk around the block.

AVIS. In these heels? Are you insane?

JASON. Avis – Could you just do something *my* way for once?

AVIS. Of course I can. You've got five minutes.

(She exits.)

ABIGAIL. I guess she's not as unreasonable as I thought.

ROGER. At least she doesn't pretend to be someone she's not.

ABIGAIL. You don't know anything about me!

*(***ABIGAIL*** exits.)*

ROGER. But I would like to, Abigail, warm caramel half moons melting on my tongue …

JASON. You've seen sounds your whole life, haven't you, Mr. Cabot?…Don't worry. I know you're not crazy.

ROGER. This from a man who pretends he's an art dealer so he can cut open my brain.

JASON. I apologize about that. But let's get one thing straight – I don't cut. I stimulate the cranial surface with lasers. There's absolutely no blood.

ROGER. What a comfort.

JASON. Let's just say I was misinformed about your condition. I know you don't see hallucinations – you really do see sounds.

ROGER. When I was a boy I thought everyone saw the world the way I did. Imagine my surprise when I realized they didn't.

JASON. So you learned to hide what you were ashamed of – to fit in…

ROGER. Just like most people do. But hiding it doesn't make it go away, does it Doctor?

JASON. Well – I – I wouldn't know about that. But I still believe I can help.

ROGER. A little brain – stimulation? Just fiddle with a few of my faulty synapses and – *(He snaps his fingers.)* I'm cured?

JASON. In a manner of speaking – yes. You won't see sounds any more, won't live in this fantasy world you've created. You can return to your normal life within a month.

ROGER. Return to my normal life? Let me explain something to you, Dr. Stewart. I know all about "normal life." I married young, went into the family business, played the game believing the game was all that mattered. That winning was all there was to life. And then I woke up.

JASON. You woke up?

ROGER. Yes. I realized after my wife died that what Thoureau said was true. "I didn't want to discover when it came time for me to die, that I had never lived..." I don't want to be the "normal" man I was, Dr. Stewart. Once I gave him up, I never wanted to go back.

JASON. Difficult as it may seem, Mr. Cabot, all of us have to make compromises to get along in this world. One of them is to at least appear normal.

ROGER. So what compromises have you made?

JASON. I don't think that's pertinent here.

ROGER. Did you ever think those compromises might be that Park Avenue condo of yours and that Mercedes and all those other things you spend your life paying for?

JASON. I made my compromises a long time ago! Now I'm reaping the rewards. That's how it works here in America, Mr. Cabot – you give up something and you get more in return.

ROGER. Sometimes we give up too much. Isn't there something you yearn for – something you had to deny yourself?

JASON. Yearn for? I don't yearn.

ROGER. All of us yearn for something. You know, saying it doesn't necessarily mean people will think you do it.

JASON. Good – because I don't do it.

ROGER. I often find it's very relieving to say things you're not thinking about doing.

JASON. Well, maybe I'll say it. Then you'll know for sure I'm not doing it.

ROGER. OK. So what *is* it you've been doing that you think seems too crazy?

JASON. That's because it *is* crazy.

ROGER. *Is?*

JASON. I mean *would be. Would be* crazy. I don't even think about it. And even if I did think about it, I certainly wouldn't talk about it, because then people would know I'd been thinking about this crazy thing and – well – it would be wrong to even think about it, so I don't – that's what we call a compromise, Mr. Cabot!

ROGER. That's what we call denial.

JASON. I don't know what you mean.

ROGER. Then what have you been doing at all those "medical conventions"?

JASON. *(looking guilty)* What do you mean what have I been doing? I've been – I've been doing – medical stuff.

ROGER. I'll tell you what you've been doing – You've been leading a secret life!

JASON. That's – that's absurd!

ROGER. You haven't been going to any medical conventions. You've been sneaking off somewhere else –

JASON. No!

ROGER. To do that crazy thing you don't ever think about, haven't you?

JASON. No! No! No! That's not true! I – I – *(suddenly breaking down)* I *do* think about it! All the time!….And I do it! Whenever I can!

ROGER. *(comforting him)* There, there. You can tell me.

JASON. Thank God! I can hardly keep it in anymore! You're right. I haven't been going to those boring medical conventions. Boring! Boring! But I couldn't let anyone, especially Avis, know what I was actually doing.

ROGER. You weren't really having an affair with Abigail, were you?

JASON. Worse than that! I was – I was – drumming.

ROGER. Drumming? As in – rock band?

JASON. No! No! As in – New Age. We sat on the floor, drumming and shaking our rattles and chanting and it blew my mind! I wanted to chuck it all – journey to the Amazon and study healing with all those wizened little old men who make you drink poison toad juice and vomit! It's crazy, I know, but I never felt so alive!

ROGER. Drink toad juice and vomit? Makes sense to me.

JASON. It does?

ROGER. If there's one thing I've learned in my last year of madness – it's never too late to change one's life.

JASON. *(gratefully)* Really? I only became a neurosurgeon to please my father.

ROGER. There seems to be a lot of that going around. *(Putting his arm around* **JASON** *and drawing him toward the French doors.)* I think we may be able to help each other. Why don't we go out into my Zen garden where we can have some privacy….By the way, you're not into thumb sucking, are you?

(They exit onto the patio.)

JASON. Thumb sucking?

RICHARD. *(entering, pausing in the doorway, upstage left, speaking to the off-tage Rebecca)* That's it, Darling. Have a good cry. Let it all out.

(He rolls his eyes and closes the off-stage room door. Then, seeing the loft is empty, he crosses to the French doors and looks out.)

That's a good boy, Jason. Looks like you're convincing the old man. Soon the Shark will be king again. And I – his heir apparent.

(There is a KNOCK on the downstage right door.)

*(***RICHARD** *crosses downstage right and opens the hall*

door revealing **THOMAS THOMAS**.)

(**THOMAS THOMAS** *is attractive and thin. He is airy, but knows the bottom line. He is gay, but not campish.* **THOMAS THOMAS** *is dressed in trendy, casual clothes.*)

RICHARD. Who the hell are you?

THOMAS. I'm an art dealer. I own a gallery in SoHo. *(handing* **RICHARD** *his business card which* **RICHARD** *reads aloud)*

RICHARD. Thomas Thomas.

THOMAS. ThoMAS ThoMAS.

(*He pronounces it "toe-MAS toe-MAS."*)

RICHARD. Sounds like a foot fungus. What do you want?

THOMAS. I would like to discuss this.

(*He begins to haul a painting in from the hall.*)

RICHARD. *Leda in Purple!?* What are you doing with that? No! Don't bring it in here! Leave it in the hall!

THOMAS. Very well.

(**THOMAS** *complies then enters fully.*)

I rescued *Leda in Purple* outside this building – from the dumpster.

RICHARD. The dumpster? I wonder how it got there?

THOMAS. I saw you dump it.

RICHARD. So what if I did dump it? It was mine to dump! That painting is an abomination! I hate it!

THOMAS. You're too critical. A perfectionist, perhaps? Well – I hope we can come to an arrangement that's satisfying for both of us.

RICHARD. Oh – I get it – you're here to talk about money, right?

THOMAS. That's why I followed you up here. *(looking around)* Are there more like *Leda?*

RICHARD. God, yes. Just look around.

(**THOMAS** *discovers the paintings against the wall and admires them.*)

If you only knew the number of Chippendale lowboys that were sold just so *Leda in Purple* could be painted. No fewer than six, I'll tell you!

THOMAS. Chippendale lowboys? I wish I had seen them. Perhaps I could have added one or two to my collection.

RICHARD. You collect Chippendale lowboys?

THOMAS. *(eyeing* **RICHARD***)* I collect all kinds of low boys.

RICHARD. Yes – well, then, you can appreciate my position – Chippendale traded for that – that naked woman!

THOMAS. The subject matter's not quite my thing either, but the technique! The exquisite use of color! The juxtaposition of – what do you want for it?

RICHARD. You want to *buy* the damn thing?

THOMAS. Don't be silly. I want to sell it. I think it could bring you a nice little sum. Say –

(He writes a figure on a small pad of paper which he has taken from his inside jacket pocket.)

What do you think of that?

RICHARD. *(looking at the paper, then speaking in shock)* **One thousand dollars**?! I can't believe this!

THOMAS. *(writing a new figure on another sheet of paper and handing it to* **RICHARD***)* Oh, all right – I'm too generous. It's my fatal flaw. What do you say to –

RICHARD. *(reading the new figure)* **Five thousand?!** Is this some sort of scam?

THOMAS. Oh – you are a wily one, you are. See right through me, don't you? All right! I'll tell you what I really want – Please – let me give you a one-man exhibition!

RICHARD. *(aghast)* What?! Really! What do you take me for? I'm engaged – to a woman!

THOMAS. We all have our idiosyncrasies. But I don't care! What can I do to convince you, Roger? Or is it – Roger?

(He pronounces the second "Roger" as if it were French.)

RICHARD. It's Roger, and there's nothing on earth that will convince me to –

THOMAS. Beg?

(He gets down on his knees.)

Is **this** what you want?

RICHARD. For God's sake! Get up before someone sees you! Did you call me "Roger"?

THOMAS. I beg you, Roger! Let me make you famous and me rich!

RICHARD. You mean – you **really** want to sell the paintings? **All** of them? For **money**?

THOMAS. That's usually what art gallery owners do...Five thousand a painting is only the beginning, Roger. I expect the price to go up rapidly.

RICHARD. Really?...Well, if everything goes as I expect... *(contemplating for a moment before speaking)* There's just one thing – I have to confess – Roger isn't my real name...My real name is – Dante.

THOMAS. Dante?

RICHARD. Yes. Dante. Dante – Ruse.

THOMAS. Dante Ruse...Gives me the shivers.

RICHARD. And don't expect me to show up for any openings or press conferences or interviews. And no photographs.

THOMAS. A man of mystery – I like that – that will drive the price up even more.

RICHARD. I'll want you to wire the money to my Swiss bank account.

THOMAS. No problem. Why don't you come by my place later, and we'll discuss the particulars. *(handing him a business card)* Here's my private number.

RICHARD. Take *Leda in Purple* with you now. I'll have the rest delivered this week.

*(**THOMAS** exits.)*

*(**REBECCA** enters. **RICHARD** quickly stuffs the card in his pocket.)*

REBECCA. Are they in the Zen garden?

RICHARD. (*crossing to look out the French doors*) It's a roof top, Rebecca. It's always been a roof top; it always will be a roof top. But it looks like Jason is convincing your father. Jason's been doing all the talking and your father just keeps nodding in agreement. I can't wait to see the old man in command again.

(**AVIS** *enters, barging in through the door downstage right.*)

REBECCA. Darling, I'm sure Jason must have explained to you that Dad won't change overnight. Psychoanalysis take years. As you well know.

AVIS. Psychoanalysis? But Jason's not a –

RICHARD. (*quickly, ushering* **AVIS** *toward the door, downstage right*) Well, it's getting late, Miss Harpinger. Why don't you wait out on the street?

AVIS. Is everyone associated with this family insane? Where's Jason?

(**RICHARD** *points to the patio.* **AVIS** *storms over to the French doors and shouts out to the patio.*)

Chez Louis now, Jason – or no more French! Ever!(*to* **REBECCA**) And he *is*, too, clumsy around me! Just this morning he dribbled some orange juice when he was pouring it.

(**ROGER** *and* **JASON** *enter through the French doors.*)

(*to* **JASON**) Are you about finished with these people?

JASON. You'll have to wait, Avis.

AVIS. (*realizing she may lose*) All right. See – I can compromise. That's what married couples do, isn't it? And Jason and I are about to be married, in case that wasn't clear to anyone here.

ROGER. I have an announcement to make. After careful consideration, and thanks to the convincing words of Dr. Stewart, I've decided to go ahead with the operation.

RICHARD. (*mouthing the words behind everyone's back*) Thank you, God!

REBECCA. *Operation?*! What operation?

JASON. I'm going to re-wire your father's brain.

REBECCA. *Re-wire my father's brain?*

AVIS. That *is* what neurosurgeons do, Miss Cabot.

REBECCA. *Neurosurgeons?*

AVIS. There seems to be an unpleasant echo in here.

REBECCA. *(to* **JASON***)* I thought you were a psychiatrist!

ROGER. God, Rebecca! Did you really think I'd let a psychiatrist mess with my brain? Maybe delusions do run in the family.

REBECCA. Richard, you never said anything about Dad having brain surgery!

RICHARD. I didn't want to overly concern you, Dearest. You know how emotional you get over little things like that.

REBECCA. But brain surgery is nothing like psychoanalysis, Dad – it's permanent!

ROGER. That's rather the point, isn't it?

REBECCA. But is it safe?

ROGER. Well, it's experimental. He does it with lasers.

RICHARD. So it doesn't really count as surgery.

REBECCA. Experimental?! Has it been tested?

JASON. Of course it's been tested. Thousands of times!

AVIS. On lab rats. And most of them lived.

REBECCA. But Dad's not a lab rat!

RICHARD. No – he's just been developing the mind of one, so it's a moot point, isn't it, Rebecca?

ROGER. Don't worry, Sweetheart. I trust Jason here completely.

REBECCA. *(to* **JASON***)* You horrible man!

JASON. *(shocked)* What? Rebecca, you don't understand!

REBECCA. My name is *Miss Cabot* to you.

AVIS. Well, now that that's settled.

> *(to* **JASON***)*

I'll meet you at Chez Louis, Darling. Don't keep me

waiting.

(She exits.)

ROGER. *(to* **REBECCA***)* Sweetheart, you should be thanking Jason. I'll be the way I used to be. That's what you want, isn't it? Oh, yes – I forgot – you don't know what you want.

REBECCA. That's not true! I do know what I want! I've thought about it and – and what I want is to save the Guatemalan Rainforest!

RICHARD. *(in horror)* Rebecca! She doesn't know what she's saying, Sir!

JASON. Oh, Rebecca! I want to save the Guatemalan Rainforest, too!

REBECCA. *(to* **JASON***)* I don't need you; I can do it all by myself! *(to* **ROGER***)* I've always wanted to save the Rainforest! – And save the whales! – And save the world! But you wouldn't let me!

*(***REBECCA** *exits, downstage right, crying.)*

JASON & RICHARD. *(rushing after her)* Rebecca! Wait!

(They collide at the doorway.)

RICHARD. *(regaining himself, speaking to* **JASON***)* I'd like you to remember she's *my* fiancee! You have Ms. Harpinger.

ROGER. Now, now – everything's going to work out just fine.

(to **RICHARD***)*

I've been wrong lately, Son, in how I've viewed you and my daughter. Yes – I was only thinking of myself. And I almost allowed something terrible to happen.

RICHARD. That's all water under the bridge, Sir.

ROGER. No, no – I want to assure my intended future son-in-law that I will remember everything you've done.

RICHARD & JASON. Thank you, Sir!

RICHARD. *(glaring at and speaking to* **JASON***)* That would be me. *(To* **ROGER***)* Thank you, Sir. I think I've earned it!

ROGER. Oh, you've earned it all right. And you're about to

get everything you deserve.
(RAPID FADE TO BLACK.)

End of Act One

ACT TWO

Scene One

(Roger's loft. One month later, close to 5 pm.)

(It is the same loft space as in Act One; however, it now has the look of a business office. The ottoman, throw pillows, sculpture chair, easel and paintings are gone. Decorative drapes hang on either side of the French doors. Upstage right, there is an office chair and a huge desk with several telephones and papers. Near the desk is another, smaller office chair and a file cabinet. A tea kettle and large wooden spoon are in the kitchen area downstage left.)

(The telephones RING.)

*(***ROGER** *stands at the desk answering the telephones. His demeanor is steely and powerful without any of the warmth or calm of the former* **ROGER.***)*

(He is dressed in an expensive business suit and tie. His hair is slicked back.)

ROGER. *(speaking alternately into the receivers)* Buy 30,000 shares at 25...Sell at 75.

*(***RICHARD** *enters, downstage right, carrying a briefcase and some suits from the dry cleaners.)*

(He is dressed similarly as in Act One.)

Hardwinkle & Snatch? Buy at 32...Sell at 80.

(noticing **RICHARD** *and speaking to him)*

Where have you been?

RICHARD. Getting your suits and those papers you –

ROGER. Excuses! Excuses!

*(**RICHARD** puts the briefcase on the desk and starts to answer one of the phones.)*

I'll get it! Just go put my suits away. Then get me a Perrier. Snap to it!

RICHARD. Yes, Sir!

*(**RICHARD** exits into the upstage left room. Once **RICHARD** is out of sight, **ROGER** winces at the sight of the ringing.)*

ROGER. *(speaking quietly and conspiratorially into the phone)* The stock market's closing right now, so all I need are just a few more calls. And space them out. The sight of all that ringing is giving me vertigo.

(The phones suddenly STOP RINGING.)

*(**RICHARD** enters and crosses into the kitchen area, upstage left.)*

*(seeing **RICHARD**, speaking impatiently into the phone, turning his back on **RICHARD**)* Next time I tell you to do something, jump to it! Or else!

*(**RICHARD** retrieves a Perrier, then, getting an idea, quietly picks up a tea kettle and a large spoon, then sneaks up behind **ROGER**.)*

No – damn-It! I won't hold!

*(**ROGER** slams down the phone. **RICHARD** suddenly bangs the spoon against the tea kettle several times quickly.)*

What the hell are you doing, Richard?

RICHARD. Do you see anything?

ROGER. As a matter of fact, I do.

RICHARD. You do?

ROGER. Yes – I see a jackass banging a tea kettle…It's been a month since the operation, Richard. Do you think that sort of thing reverses itself? I'm back, and I'm here to stay!

RICHARD. Yes, Sir!

(He quickly hands the Perrier to **ROGER**.*)*

Your Perrier, Sir.

ROGER. Who in the hell has time for Perrier? Did you get a response from Adam Parnell?

RICHARD. He absolutely refuses to sell. And nothing I can say will change his mind.

ROGER. That's funny. You seemed to have a great influence over Adam when the two of you were conspiring to take over my company this past year.

RICHARD. What? You have to believe me – I wasn't thinking about myself. I was torn up by the thought the other employees would lose their jobs if the company went under. I'm sentimental that way.

ROGER. That's just the kind of bleeding heart crap I can't stomach. First rule of business – what's good for the company is not always good for the employees. In fact, it's best not to consider the employees at all. They can always be replaced – get my meaning?

RICHARD. I think I do. The take-over scheme was all Adam's idea.

ROGER. Really? I admire that kind of treachery –

RICHARD. You do? Well, in truth, I helped develop it into a full-fledged scheme. As a matter of fact –

ROGER. – when it's done to someone *other* than me.

RICHARD. Oh…But you weren't yourself – were you, Sir? And now that you are yourself, we both know you can convince Adam to sell his company. Use your old charm.

ROGER. Yes. I know just how to grab Adam Parnell by the balls.

RICHARD. Just like old times.

ROGER. By the way – do you know someone named Dante Ruse?

RICHARD. Dante Ruse? Never heard of him. Never. Why?

ROGER. I got a strange phone call this morning from some French woman asking for this Dante guy. I told her no such person lived here. When I tried to question her further, she hung up.

RICHARD. I wouldn't pay any attention, Sir. Probably some scam.

ROGER. Funny thing is – I seem to recall that name – Dante – Dante –

RICHARD. It's a fairly common name. You know, I think Rebecca's planning on stopping by.

ROGER. Rebecca?

RICHARD. Your daughter, Sir. My fiancee.

ROGER. Oh, yes.

(*He hands some files to* **RICHARD**.)

Don't just stand there. Make yourself useful. File these contracts.

(**RICHARD** *begins filing, his back to the downstage left hall door.*)

I still can't believe my little baby girl is tying the knot next month. Why it seems like only yesterday she got her first job.

RICHARD. That *was* only yesterday.

(**REBECCA** *enters through the hall door, downstage left.* **RICHARD** *does not see her, but* **ROGER** *does. She is dressed in much freer clothing than before. Her hair is loose.*)

I still don't understand Rebecca's desire to work for an hourly wage.

ROGER. I believe she said something about wanting the satisfaction of making it on her own.

RICHARD. Whatever that means. But don't worry, Sir. All that will change once we're married. She won't be going around photographing any more toxic dumpsites for that "Save The Earth" newsletter.

REBECCA. Hello, Richard.

RICHARD. (*turning to her, startled*) Darling! Have you finally picked out a wedding dress?

REBECCA. No. I – I haven't decided yet.

RICHARD. The wedding date's fast approaching, Sweetheart. Might want to get that resolved.

ROGER. At least before you save the world. How's that coming, by the way?

REBECCA. Just fine. I've started with New Jersey.

ROGER. New Jersey? Why start at the bottom? I'll give you a big, fat salary, a river-view office, two months of vacation, and you won't have to do a thing.

REBECCA. That's what I've been doing all my life – not a thing!

ROGER. And you've been so good at it, I think you ought to make a career out of it.

REBECCA. Well, I'm not going to do it any more! *(Taking a check from her purse and handing it to* **ROGER.**) Here, Dad.

ROGER. What's this?

REBECCA. My allowance for this month. I don't want it.

RICHARD. Rebecca! Is that any way to speak to your father?

ROGER. What's this silliness? Turning up your nose at the family fortune? Why do you think I worked so hard all those years?

RICHARD. Yes, Rebecca! Hasn't your father taught you anything? We will accept your money, Sir.

REBECCA. No I won't! I don't want his money. It's kept me a prisoner all these years.

ROGER. A prisoner? Poor thing! Forced to eat caviar and smoked salmon. Nothing but private schools and trips to Europe. For God's sake, Rebecca – what *do* you want? Oh, that's right – to save the world and the whales. Maybe I will take that check back.

RICHARD. *(taking the check)* Let me hold it for you, Sir.

(One of the phones RINGS.)

ROGER. *(answering the phone)* Speak up! I don't have all day! *(pause)* I don't care if it takes red hot tongs. Resort to kidnapping if you have to. *(pause)* Not her kid – her dog! She loves that thing.

(*He turns his back and continues to speak quietly on the phone.*)

RICHARD. It's a beautiful sight, isn't it?

REBECCA. If you like icebergs. My other Dad was more – human.

RICHARD. Well it's a good thing we nipped that in the bud.

REBECCA. Richard, I have something personal to talk to you about – in private.

RICHARD. Of course, Dear. Call my secretary and make an appointment. I'm sure I can fit you in next week.

REBECCA. Not next week. Now.

RICHARD. Now? Well, I'm rather busy at the moment.

REBECCA. I'm getting cold feet about our marriage.

RICHARD. What?! Cold feet? You can't mean it!

REBECCA. We can discuss it on the patio, if you want.

(**REBECCA** *exits quickly onto the patio.*)

RICHARD. Rebecca! Wait!

(*He whines and shakes his head and hands as he exits onto the patio.*)

(*There is a KNOCK on the downstage right door.* **ROGER** *hangs up the phone and crosses to open the downstage right door, revealing* **JASON.**)

JASON. (*entering*) Is she here? I've got to see her! I've got to speak to her!

ROGER. Rebecca's on the patio with Dick. I'm pleased to report she's beginning to show some guts. Richard, on the other hand, still thinks he'd do anything to become me. Poor boy. I feel responsible. I taught him everything he knows. Now I've got to show him the error of his ways.

JASON. But I can't stand it any more! Rebecca won't meet with me! She won't return any of my phone calls! She thinks I'm some sort of Dr. Frankenstein for changing you! Which I didn't!

ROGER. Stop right there, Jason. You can't tell her you didn't really operate on me. Not yet, at least.

JASON. But why not?

ROGER. Rebecca is still engaged to Richard. Nothing has changed that – yet. And you're still engaged to Avis, aren't you?

JASON. Avis? Oh, yes – her. My mother taught me an engagement is a pledge that can't be broken lightly – no matter how much you've changed – or who you love.

ROGER. Well if things aren't allowed to change any further, you and Rebecca will marry your fiancees and have no reason to speak to each other ever again.

JASON. Well, I don't want her to remember me as someone she should forget.

ROGER. Patience, Jason. Good things come to those who wait. And remember – Rebecca has a forgiving heart. By the way, how are you doing with the drumming?

JASON. Great. Except it's getting harder and harder to hide it from Avis. Just last week she almost caught me pounding away in my office.

(**REBECCA** *enters, followed by* **RICHARD**.)

RICHARD. *(to* **REBECCA***)* What if we see a marriage counselor before the wedding?

JASON. *(seeing* **REBECCA**, *starry-eyed)* Rebecca …

(*He bumps into a lamp and hastily rights it.*)

REBECCA. *(coolly)* Doctor Stewart.

ROGER. Jason just dropped by to see how I was doing, isn't that right, Jason?

JASON. Yes – right.

(*One of the phones RINGS.*)

ROGER. *(answering the phone)* What is it? *(turning his back on them to talk privately)*

JASON. *(to* **REBECCA***)* Congratulations on your upcoming wedding. You must be very happy.

REBECCA. Obviously my happiness is none of your concern, Doctor Stewart.

JASON. But Rebecca! Your happiness is all I think about! I'd like to explain everything –

REBECCA. Ok. Explain everything.

(**ROGER** *glares at* **JASON**.)

JASON. – if only I could.

REBECCA. Oh!

(*She exits onto the patio.*)

JASON. Rebecca! Wait!

(*He exits onto the patio after her just as* **THOMAS** *appears in the downstage right doorway.* **RICHARD** *spots* **THOMAS** *and crosses quickly to him.*)

RICHARD. Thomas! I told you not to come here!

THOMAS. (*entering, scanning the loft in shock*) What's happened to your studio?

RICHARD. (*pulling* **THOMAS** *aside and whispering to him*) I – uh – I'm being evicted.

THOMAS. (*whispering*) Evicted? But I need more paintings! My clients are wild about you!

RICHARD. (*whispering*) You know I've been painting every night for the past two weeks until four in the morning! I've given you three new paintings already – *Leda in Red, Leda in White, Leda in Yellow*! What more do you want?

THOMAS. (*whispering*) I want you to paint more. That's what artists do, isn't it?

RICHARD. (*whispering*) God, you're so demanding!

ROGER. (*cradling the phone he's been speaking into against his chest and speaking about* **THOMAS**) Who the hell is this?

RICHARD. (*explaining to* **ROGER**) He's – uh – he's here to – um – to get some rocks off on the patio.

THOMAS. I thought you'd never ask.

ROGER. Well, make it quick.

THOMAS. We'll try.

RICHARD. *(grabbing* **THOMAS** *by the arm and draws him toward the French doors)* Just come on.

THOMAS. You artists! So impulsive!

*(***RICHARD*** thrusts* **THOMAS** *through the French doorway just as* **REBECCA** *reenters from the patio followed by* **JASON.** *)*

RICHARD. *(whining as he shakes his head and hands)* Ohhh-hhh …

*(***JASON*** stares at* **RICHARD** *as he exits.)*

REBECCA. It's his way of releasing tension.

JASON. You're so understanding.

REBECCA. I am *not* understanding! I used to be understanding, but not anymore!

ROGER. *(shouting into the phone)* Sue the bastard! Make him sweat! I don't care if he is only twelve! These computer geeks! Nail him to the wall!

REBECCA. Look at him! *You've* made him a monster!

JASON. But I didn't! Rebecca! Please!

REBECCA. Don't give me your excuses! All I want is for you to change him back!

JASON. But I can't!

REBECCA. Then I hate you!

(She exits onto the patio.)

JASON. Rebecca!

(He exits after her as **RICHARD** *and* **THOMAS** *enter through the French doors.)*

THOMAS. *(quietly, so that only* **RICHARD** *can hear)* So it's settled – you'll come to my apartment tonight – with another painting?

RICHARD. *(whispering to* **THOMAS** *as he ushers him to the downstage right door)* All right! All right! Now would you just go!

THOMAS. You temperamental artists. I love it!

(**THOMAS** *exits downstage right as* **RICHARD** *stares, pre-occupied, after him.*)

ROGER. *(into phone)* Just do it!

(*He hangs up as* **REBECCA** *enters with* **JASON** *following.*)

JASON. *(to* **REBECCA***)* Maybe we could have lunch sometime? Just the two of us? I would like to tell you –

ROGER. I'm afraid not, Jason. That would look unseemly. She's about to be a married woman, you know.

(*slapping* **RICHARD** *on the back*)

Isn't that right, Richard?

RICHARD. *(startled, having not followed the previous conversation)* What?

ROGER. Get with it, son! You're not going to let some male meddle with your manhood, are you?

RICHARD. No! Of course not! No one meddles with my manhood!

ROGER. *(pushing* **RICHARD** *into* **REBECCA***'s arms)* Then show Jason how happy you two are together!

(**REBECCA** *and* **RICHARD** *kiss tentatively and chastely.*)

There! Doesn't that look happy?

JASON. Not really.

REBECCA. Oh – why don't you just go away!

AVIS. *(entering)* Jason! Darling! There you are!

(*She is dressed very sexily, but tastefully.*)

JASON. Avis, what are you doing here?

AVIS. *(crossing to* **JASON***, and draping herself on him)* I followed you, of course, Silly.

JASON. *(trying to extricate himself from* **AVIS***)* This following me around is getting a bit much, Avis.

AVIS. This is what I'm like when I'm in love – impatient, impetuous, impassioned!

ROGER. *(to himself)* Impossible.

(to **AVIS***)*

Miss Harpinger– It's as much a pleasure to see you as it always is.

AVIS. *(kissing* **JASON***'s ear)* At least someone misses me.

ROGER. As perceptive as you are charming, I see.

JASON. *(finally pulling away from* **AVIS***)* Avis, please!

AVIS. Don't be so prudish, Jason. Rebecca must know what abandoning oneself to pure, sexual desire is like. I'm sure she and Richard have had a similar experience, isn't that right, Rebecca?

REBECCA. Dozens of times. All sorts of places and positions, so numerous I can't count them all, let alone remember even one.

ROGER. Yes, I'm sure Richard is an absolute wild man when unleashed.

RICHARD. I am?

AVIS. This place certainly has changed. What a difference sanity makes. What happened to all those paintings?

ROGER. Paintings?

AVIS. You know – rectangular things you hang on the wall. *(to* **JASON***)* I thought you said he was all better?

RICHARD. I got rid of those ghastly paintings.

AVIS. Really? *You* got rid of them?

RICHARD. Mr. Cabot no longer indulges in that sort of thing. And he wishes to forget he ever did.

AVIS. Well I saw some very interesting paintings quite like them in a gallery in SoHo —

RICHARD. *(quickly escorting* **AVIS** *and* **JASON** *to the dowbstage right door)* Yes, yes. Well, Jason was just leaving. *(to* **JASON***)* Isn't that right, Jason? Your operation was such a big success. No need for either of you to ever come back. Mr. Cabot's been returned to the man we all wanted.

AVIS. How nice. So everyone has the man they all want.

*(***AVIS** *stares adoringly at* **JASON***, then with a look of annoyance, notices that* **JASON** *is looking longingly at*

REBECCA *who sadly glances from* ROGER *to* RICHARD. RICHARD *stares after the departed* THOMAS.)

(One of the phones RINGS.)

ROGER. Get that, Richard. Hurry up!

(RICHARD *answers the phone and* ROGER *begins reading some papers from his desk.)*

REBECCA. *(to* JASON*)* You and your fiancee had just better go.

AVIS. *(to* JASON*)* Shall we?

JASON. *(sadly, to* REBECCA*)* It's good-bye, then?

(He and AVIS *exit.)*

REBECCA. *(shouting after* JASON*)* And good riddance!

(to ROGER*)*

I guess I'll be leaving, too, Dad....Dad?

ROGER. *(preoccupied, not looking up)* Whatever.

REBECCA. *(Pausing for a moment, hoping for an emotional response from* ROGER*)* Dad?...I thought maybe you and I could go out to dinner later?

ROGER. *(still preoccupied with the papers)* Damn it! Down ten points! How did I miss that?

REBECCA. Or if you're busy, I could always go home and slit my wrists.

ROGER. *(still concentrating on the papers)* Yes – fine, fine. Have a nice day.

(RICHARD *hangs up the phone as* REBECCA, *near tears, exits, DR.* ROGER *glances up.)*

Now that they're all gone – Back to business. Can I really trust you, son?

RICHARD. Of course, Sir!

ROGER. Good. Now that you're going to be a member of the family, I want you to know everything so that you can carry on when I'm gone.

RICHARD. When you're gone? Are you ill, Sir? I mean, is it terminal? Less than three months to live? That sort of thing?

ROGER. I'm as healthy as a horse!

RICHARD. Oh….Well, then – Tell me how you do it. How do you get a bastard like Adam Parnell to crumble to his knees?

ROGER. Blackmail.

RICHARD. Blackmail?

ROGER. Yes – I want you to get some pictures of the very married Mr. Parnell in a compromising position with someone other than his wife.

RICHARD. Adam's having an affair? I never even suspected the old dog.

ROGER. That's because he's *not* having an affair. He's faithfully married. You'll have to create the scene, if you get my drift.

RICHARD. *I'll* have to create the scene? You mean – a *sex* scene? But where am I going to find that kind of woman?

ROGER. Who said anything about a woman?

RICHARD. You mean –?! I never knew Adam was –!

ROGER. He's *not*. Richard – get with it. Just because a man leads an unblemished personal life doesn't mean we can't ruin him by changing that perception.

RICHARD. Oh – I get it. Pretty clever, Mr. Cabot.

ROGER. So if Adam were to – say – meet an attractive woman –

RICHARD. *(getting into it)* Who was really a man just disguised as a woman –

ROGER. And who lured him to some hotel room –

RICHARD. And we got the pictures…But where are we going to find a man willing to dress up like a woman and lure – ?

(ROGER stares at RICHARD.)

You mean – you want *me* –?! To –?! With *Adam*?!

ROGER. *(speaking as he writes on a slip of paper)* You don't have to actually *do* anything. Just get the pictures.

(He hands RICHARD the piece of paper.)

Here's the number of a private detective I've used

before.

(**RICHARD** *reluctantly takes the slip of paper.* **ROGER** *pulls a shopping bag out from behind the desk. He takes out a, sexy, red satin dress from the bag and crosses to* **RICHARD**. *He holds the dress up to* **RICHARD**.)

What do you think?

RICHARD. (*unenthusiastically taking the dress*) Couldn't you hire a professional for this?

ROGER. And give someone I don't trust the ammunition to blackmail me? I don't think so. Go ahead – let's see if it fits.

RICHARD. I – I can't!

ROGER. Why not? Red isn't your color?

RICHARD. No! I mean – yes! I mean – I can't wear a dress in public!

ROGER. (*while he removes a blonde wig from the bag*) Sure you can. Here…

(*He tosses the wig at* **RICHARD** *who catches it.*)

Adam's partial to blondes. Let's see how it looks.

(**RICHARD** *reluctantly puts on the wig. It is askew.*)

Not like that!

(**ROGER** *crosses to* **RICHARD** *and adjusts the wig, then appraises his work.*)

There. A little bit of lipstick…A little bit of foundation – that cologne you're wearing will do nicely.

(**RICHARD** *looks depressed as* **ROGER** *crosses to the shopping bag.*)

Don't worry. You're a natural.

RICHARD. A natural what?

ROGER. Conniver – just like the old man, here. What did you think I meant? Oh – and Adam's quite fond of spike heels.

(*He pulls out a pair of spike heels from the bag.*)

RICHARD. *(throwing the dress down and pulling off the wig)* I can't! I absolutely refuse to wear this – this – this get-up. It's simply not acceptable!

ROGER. Come on – You'll do fine. *(handing* **RICHARD** *a slip of paper)* Just go to this address tomorrow night at eight–

RICHARD. No! No! No! I won't dress up like a woman! I won't! Never! End of discussion! If you want to get Adam Parnell, you'll have to do it some other way!

ROGER. I can see you really mean this.

RICHARD. Nothing could ever make me change my mind.

ROGER. Well, if that's the way you feel…It's too bad, really. I had big plans for you, Richard.

RICHARD. You did? Big plans?

ROGER. Big, big plans…But – I guess it is your choice – isn't it?

(BLACKOUT.)

End of Scene One

Scene Two

(Roger's loft. Late evening the next day.)

(The loft is as in Scene One, except that a pair of Roger's pants is hanging over the back of the desk chair. The room is lit with a soft light. Chinese MUSIC is heard.)

(ROGER is doing T'ai Chi. He is dressed in boxer shorts and a white dress shirt. The intercom BUZZES.)

ROGER. *(wincing at the image the sound makes and trying to wipe it away)* Agh! I hate that yellow slash!

(He quickly crosses to the computer and turns off the music. The MUSIC stops. The intercom BUZZES again.)

All right! All right! (*quickly crossing to the intercom and speaking into it*) What do you want?

ABIGAIL. *(over the intercom)* It's me. May I come up? I need to speak to you.

ROGER. *(speaking into the intercom)* Dr. Stewart's ghostwriter, is it? Suit yourself.

(He buzzes her in, then puts on the pants hanging over the back of the desk chair. There is a knock at the door, downstage right.)

(He crosses to the door downstage right and opens it wide, revealing **ABIGAIL**, *who enters. She is dressed casually, but tastefully.)*

So what brings our esteemed journalist sniffing around? Got a hot tip that Elvis was sighted on the patio?

ABIGAIL. There's something I felt you should know. Richard Borman conned your daughter into agreeing to your operation. It wasn't her idea at all. In fact – she didn't even know there was going to be an operation. And Jason didn't know that she didn't know – or that you didn't know, although in the end, you did seem to know. But Richard knew everything from the beginning. I just wanted to make that perfectly clear.

ROGER. Thank you for that deft explanation. What about you? What did you know?

ABIGAIL. I knew Jason intended to operate if he could get your consent. But that was before I'd met you. If I'd met you first, I wouldn't have wanted to – to –

ROGER. To cure me?

ABIGAIL. To change anything about you.

ROGER. Well, I am cured. And I have Richard *and* you to thank…If this little revelation is why you came, you could have saved yourself the trouble and phoned first.

ABIGAIL. I thought you didn't have a telephone.

ROGER. Not have a telephone? I know you write for a tabloid, but are you a complete idiot? I need to conduct business, don't I? *(holding up a phone)* What do you think I do with this?

ABIGAIL. I have a suggestion.

ROGER. Well, unless there's some other reason you've come –?

ABIGAIL. Say my name.

ROGER. I beg your pardon.

ABIGAIL. Just humor me. Say my name.

ROGER. I'm sorry, but what is your name?

ABIGAIL. Don't you remember?

ROGER. No. I seem to have forgotten.

ABIGAIL. It's Abigail.

ROGER. All right. Here goes – Ab-i-gail. There. I said it. Now what?

ABIGAIL. Did anything happen?

ROGER. Happen? What? Is the earth supposed to move?

ABIGAIL. Yes – I was hoping it would. Or at least rumble.

ROGER. Usually that's the first sign of a disaster.

ABIGAIL. What's happened to you?

ROGER. You know precisely what's happened to me – you were in on it – Dr. Jason Stewart's magical brain cure.

What did you expect by coming here? That I'd recall some emotion growing between you and the old Roger?

ABIGAIL. There was something between us.

ROGER. Do you really believe he thought of you as any different from the models who paraded through that door? After all, you'd only met him for a few minutes.

ABIGAIL. *(barely containing her anger)* And I've only met the new Roger for about five minutes, but I already dislike you intensely.

ROGER. Thank you, but surely, being a "journalist," you can come up with a better choice of words. "You make me want to puke," for instance.

ABIGAIL. Too mild. How about I loathe you?

ROGER. Better.

ABIGAIL. *(her voice rising angrily)* I detest you!

ROGER. Now you're getting it.

(He approaches her.)

ABIGAIL. Despise! Abhor! Hate you! The Roger I knew was warm and exciting. You're – nothing like him.

ROGER. If you want warmth, I suggest you get a puppy dog. And if you want excitement –

(He grabs her, pulling her to him.)

I'm the only Roger Cabot you could ever want.

(He kisses her passionately and she responds with equal passion.)

Abigail – let me confess – I'm –

*(**RICHARD** enters suddenly, but covertly, unaware of Abigail's presence. He is dressed in drag – wearing the blonde wig, the red, satin dress, one of the black high heels, and make up. He carries an evening bag and the other high heel, which is broken. He looks a bit disheveled.)*

RICHARD. God, I hope no one saw – *(Spotting **ABIGAIL**, he changes his voice to a falsetto.)* me! What's she doing here?

ABIGAIL. *(to* **ROGER***)* Who's this? Your date?

ROGER.	**RICHARD.**
No!	Yes.

RICHARD. I mean – no?

ROGER. If I told you, you wouldn't believe it.

ABIGAIL. Try me.

ROGER. Well – uh – Abigail, this is – um – um –

ABIGAIL. Um – um what?

RICHARD. *(in falsetto)* Just Um-Um.

ROGER. Yes! Just Um-Um. It's Ancient Phoenician.

ABIGAIL. Right. Please to meet you – Um-Um.

RICHARD. *(in falsetto)* Charmed, I'm sure.

ROGER. Um-Um just started working for me – as my – my – as my secretary.

ABIGAIL. Your secretary? Right. She must be an expert at handling your phone.

RICHARD. *(in falsetto)* I happen to be quite good at typing.

ROGER. And dictation…

RICHARD. *(in falsetto)* And filing…

ABIGAIL. And lying?

RICHARD. *(in falsetto)* Yes. I mean – no! I mean – *(To* **ROGER***)* What's the right answer?

ROGER. Shut up.

ABIGAIL. I can see your company has a strict dress code.

ROGER. Friday is dress down day.

ABIGAIL. Finally something I can believe. Tell me – why is your secretary here at 11 p.m. – with her own key to *your* loft?

ROGER. She's – delivering some very important papers.

RICHARD. *(in falsetto)* Top secret.

ABIGAIL. *(noticing that* **RICHARD** *only carries a small purse)* Really? I wonder where she's concealing them? Or maybe that's part of the Roger Uncovers Secret Papers game? Bet that cost extra.

RICHARD. *(in falsetto, insulted)* What do you take me for?!

(A cell phone in Richard's purse rings.)

Excuse me. *(pulling the phone from the purse and answering in falsetto)* Hello?

(In a whisper, in his normal voice, so that **ROGER** *and* **ABIGAIL** *can't hear)*

Thomas?…No, it's me. I have a cold.

ROGER. You don't understand, Abigail. Um-Um here must have forgotten the papers. *(to* **RICHARD***)* Isn't that right, Um-Um?

RICHARD. *(in falsetto, to* **ABIGAIL***)* What? Oh, yes. Silly me! *(in his normal voice, whispering into the phone, so* **ROGER** *and* **ABIGAIL** *can't hear)* No, Thomas! You can't tell the Times who I really am!

ABIGAIL. Do you think I'm a blind idiot?

ROGER. Of course not.

ABIGAIL. If you want to date a tart –

RICHARD. *(in falsetto, to* **ABIGAIL***)* Tart?! *(into the phone, in his normal voice so that* **ROGER** *and* **ABIGAIL** *can't hear)* Not you!

ABIGAIL. *(to* **ROGER***)* If you want to date *whatever* – it's your business. I'm just sorry I ever met you!

(She exits hurriedly, downstage right.)

ROGER. *(exiting after her)* Abigail! Wait!

RICHARD. *(speaking into the phone at first with trepidation, then with increasing enthusiasm)* Yes, I know the painting I did last night isn't a *Leda.* I just couldn't bear to do another one. *(pause)* I know I've gone in an entirely new direction. I was hoping you'd like it. *(pause)* What? *(pause)* Oh, Thomas! You love it? Do you really mean it? Because it's my own! I mean it's really my own! And I like it! I really, really, really like it! *(pause)* Yes, I'm already working on another one.

ROGER. *(entering, sadly to himself)* Abigail – Warm caramel half-moons melting on my tongue…

RICHARD. *(whispering into the phone)* Look, I've got to go.... Yes, I'll see you later. And Thomas – I'm really glad you like the new painting.

*(He hangs up. Speaking in falsetto to **ROGER** as he removes the wig.)*

Thank God – *(returning to his normal voice)* Thank God she's gone! Do you think she recognized me?

(He begins wiping the make-up off his face with a hand-kerchief.)

ROGER. No. You're very convincing. But you look a bit of a mess. How did it go with Adam?

RICHARD. *(speaking agitatedly while he strips down to his boxer shorts and dresses in his own clothes)* How did it go? Well, let's see – I patiently waited for Adam who, by the way, didn't show up at eight, like you said he would. But three or four near-sighted drunks at the hotel lounge thought I was a very attractive woman, if that counts. Why else would they have tackled that undercover officer who was chasing me? Of course, that was after I'd nearly been arrested for solicitation, but before the brawl. By then there were so many arms and legs flying that I wouldn't have noticed even if Adam had jumped on my back and shouted "Giddyap!" I just took off running and nearly broke my ankle in these insane high heels! ***That's*** how it went! Why I ever let you talk me into this – this ridiculous costume, I don't know!

ROGER. *(trying to conceal his laughter)* It was your choice to go through with it, Richard. I'm just kind of surprised you did.

RICHARD. I'm not sure I'm cut out for corporate life.

ROGER. You can always quit. Give it all up, like I once did.

RICHARD. I'm not that crazy yet. So what do we do now since we didn't get those pictures?

ROGER. Yes – what to do about Adam…

RICHARD. Corporate espionage? Dig up scandals about the board? Bribe the stockholders? As long as it doesn't involve any more disguises.

ROGER. You're such a tenderfoot, Richard. Tactics like that leave too many loose ends – too many witnesses who might testify, if you know what I mean?

RICHARD. Oh, yes – I read you perfectly.

ROGER. Good. Then I know I can count on you.

RICHARD. Of course! What do you want me to do?

ROGER. (taking a handgun from his desk drawer and handing to RICHARD who backs away) Kill him.

RICHARD. *Kill* him? You mean – *kill Adam?*

ROGER. You don't have a problem with that, do you?

RICHARD. Me?…Oh, no! Why should I have a problem with that? Why would anyone have a problem with that? It's just that –

ROGER. Just that what?

RICHARD. It seems rather extreme.

ROGER. Richard, you're not going to go all weak-kneed on me, are you? It takes guts and nerve to succeed in this business. Not heart and soul. Do you have what it takes?

RICHARD. Couldn't we try negotiating?

ROGER. The time for negotiating is over! Now it's time for action!

RICHARD. Is this the secret of your success, Sir? Killing all of your competitors?

ROGER. I don't limit myself to just competitors. Anyone who irritates me – pfff!

RICHARD. Pfff?

ROGER. Take that McDougal fellow who used to be in Marketing.

RICHARD. Paul McDougal? I thought he was on vacation in Bali – expenses paid by the company.

ROGER. Well you could say he's taking a long rest, but I'm not sure he'd classify it as a company perk.

RICHARD. But wasn't he promoted to the Thirteenth floor?

ROGER. Son – the company only has *twelve* floors.

RICHARD. What did McDougal do?

ROGER. What did he *do*? Why he threatened the company's financial stability – that's what he did! Managed to undermine the *entire* company's image of wholesomeness – the kind of image that *sells* to all those gullible consumers out there.

RICHARD. How could one man do all that?

ROGER. He wore a skirt to the company picnic, the pantywaist!

RICHARD. A skirt? The company picnic? No – Sir – you're mistaken. It was a kilt.

ROGER. You add an "s" and change the "l" to an "r" and a kilt is nothing more than a skirt in disguise. You of all people should know that. When you undermine the company's image, what happens, Richard?

RICHARD. You're terminated.

ROGER. Correct.

RICHARD. But I thought terminated meant fired! Not killed!

ROGER. We have to uphold the image of family values at this company. Here. It's already loaded.

(**ROGER** *hands the gun to* **RICHARD** *who backs away from it.*)

RICHARD. Loaded?

ROGER. It's a bit hard to kill someone with an unloaded gun – although I guess you could bonk him on the head a couple of times.

RICHARD. But I've never killed anyone before!

ROGER. Look at me, Richard. Why do you think I'm where I am today?

RICHARD. Not enough funding for police?

ROGER. Guts and nerve, Richard. Guts and nerve. You wanted to be just like me – here's your chance. Or would you rather work for an hourly wage?

RICHARD. An hourly wage?!

ROGER. You could live in a tiny one-room apartment – get rid of all those antiques you've collected. And take the subway to work.

RICHARD. The *subway*?!

ROGER. Packed in like a sardine with all those sweaty, little people. And before you go, maybe the company would send *you* to Bali.

RICHARD. To Bali?!

ROGER. As a farewell present.

(**RICHARD** *quickly takes the gun.*)

Glad you're seeing things my way.

(**RICHARD** *reluctantly begins to exit.*)

But first –

RICHARD. *(stopping)* There's **more**?

ROGER. Do you remember those paintings I used to do?

RICHARD. Isn't it best to forget unpleasant things?

(**ROGER** *glares at him.*)

Sir! You were mad when you painted them! Mad! You said so yourself.

ROGER. You're right, Richard. But it seems that some bastard has found those paintings and is passing them off as his own. And do you know who that bastard is?

RICHARD. Who?

ROGER. Someone named Dante Ruse.

RICHARD. Dante Ruse?

ROGER. Ring a bell? *(pause)* That strange phone call two weeks ago? That French woman asking for Dante Ruse?

RICHARD. Do you have any idea who this Dante Ruse is?

ROGER. No. I want you to find out.

RICHARD. Me?

ROGER. And when you do, I want you to kill him.

RICHARD. You want me to kill Dante Ruse? Before I kill

Adam Parnell or after?

ROGER. Before. We can't risk anyone finding out that I painted those paintings. And besides, I can't let anyone dupe me. I've got my reputation to think of.

RICHARD. Wouldn't want to discredit that.

ROGER. The gun's been stolen, and the serial number's been filed off. Still, you might want to wear gloves. And use some discretion. We don't want witnesses turning up.

RICHARD. Witnesses?

ROGER. Then you'd have to kill them, and things get complicated.

RICHARD. Any other words of advice before I commit my first capital offense?

(**ROGER** *escorts* **RICHARD** *to the door, downstage right.*)

ROGER. Cheer up, Richard. It's only business. The Wolf of Wallstreet – on the prowl!

(**ROGER** *lets out a howl while* **RICHARD** *shakes his hands and head and lets out a whine.*)

(*FADE to BLACK*)

End of Scene Two

Scene Three

(Roger's loft. The next evening. The loft is as in the last scene. The room is lit.)

*(**RICHARD** enters downstage right, in a very agitated state. He pulls the gun from his coat pocket and throws it on the desk)*

RICHARD. Oh, God! What have I done?

(He notices with horror that there is something on his tie)

Oh, God! Is it –? It is! Cadmium Red! I knew I should have worn a smock!

(He rubs furiously at his tie, examines it again, then rubs some more, even more furiously.)

Out! Out, damned spot!

*(**ROGER** enters, unnoticed by **RICHARD**, from the patio.)*

ROGER. Richard?

RICHARD. *(startled)* Ah!

ROGER. Get a grip! It's only me!

RICHARD. How reassuring.

ROGER. *(noticing the stained tie)* What's that on your tie?

RICHARD. On my tie…?

ROGER. That red spot. Is it – ?

RICHARD. Blood! – Yes! It's blood! Dante Ruse's blood!

ROGER. Dante Ruse's blood? You've killed him? With that gun?

RICHARD. Hunted him down and gave it to him – right between the –

(The intercom BUZZES.)

ROGER. Balls!

RICHARD. I was going to say "eyes."

ROGER. I forgot I invited that swindling little twerp of an art dealer who connived with Dante Ruse to meet me here.

RICHARD. Thomas? Here?

ROGER. Hey – why don't you take care of him while you're here?

RICHARD. *(fearfully)* When you say "take care of," do you mean "take care of"? or do you mean, "take care of"?

ROGER. *(putting the gun in **RICHARD**'s hand)* Take care of the way you took care of Dante. Don't look so glum, Richard. It's easier after the first time.

(The intercom BUZZES again.)

Well?

RICHARD. All right. Fine. I'll take care of him. But maybe you should wait on the patio until I'm done. Wouldn't want any witnesses, would we?

ROGER. Now you're catching on.

*(**ROGER** exits onto the patio, closing the doors behind him.)*

RICHARD. *(answering the intercom, whispering)* Go away! We don't want any!

AVIS. *(over the intercom, disguising her voice with a French accent)* Monsieur, I am looking for an artist who is at this address.

RICHARD. Wrong apartment!

AVIS. *(still with a French accent)* He owes me money for posing naked, and I will make a big fuss until I collect.

RICHARD. *(after a brief pause, into the intercom)* Oh – come up.

(He buzzes her up, then pulls out his wallet and looks through the bills.)

It's bad enough I have to paint his damn paintings – now I have to pay his damn models…Oh crap! I hope she takes American Express.

*(There is a KNOCK heard on the door, downstage right. **RICHARD** crosses to the door and opens it, revealing **AVIS**.)*

Avis!

(He glances behind her in the hall to see if anyone else

is there.)

Did anyone come up with you?

AVIS. No.

RICHARD. You didn't see a woman out there?

AVIS. Are you all right, Richard?

RICHARD. Why shouldn't I be all right? What could possibly be wrong?

AVIS. I don't know. Why do you have that gun?

RICHARD. *(tossing the gun on the desk)* What gun? It's not mine! In fact, I've never seen that gun before in my life! And if I had seen it before, I certainly wouldn't know how to use it! Couldn't use it! Didn't use it!

AVIS. What's going on? Come on, you can tell me, Richard. There's nothing to be afraid of.

RICHARD. You haven't seen Roger Cabot lately.

AVIS. Where is Roger?

RICHARD. Believe me – you don't want to know. Let's just say I got rid of him.

AVIS. What do you mean you got rid of him?

RICHARD. Do you see him?

AVIS. No.

RICHARD. That's because he's gone. No longer with us. Get it?

AVIS. Departed?

RICHARD. Yes! Departed! *(to himself)* My God, lawyers can be so exacting sometimes. *(speaking to her as he ushers her toward the door)* Perhaps you could come back another time.

AVIS. *(seeing the red stain on his tie, horrified)* Is that – ? Is that – *blood*?

(As she reaches out to touch the spot, **RICHARD** *backs away.)*

RICHARD. Of course it's not blood! Why would I have blood on my tie? I wouldn't! Couldn't! Didn't! Didn't do anything!

AVIS. You've killed him, haven't you? You've killed Roger Cabot.

RICHARD. *(He starts to laugh insanely.)* Now there's a thought. *(coming to his senses)* Of course I haven't killed Roger Cabot! **He** gave me that gun and ordered me to kill someone else! In fact – a couple of someone elses. And I've succeeded! Totally and completely!…In failing! And this is not blood on my tie! It's oil paint!

AVIS. Oil paint. Right. Now I've heard them all.

*(**AVIS** touches the spot on his tie and looks closely, then smells the finger with which she touched the tie.)*

It **is** oil paint.

RICHARD. Don't you lawyers ever listen to the truth? After Roger gave me my orders I found myself wandering the streets imagining what my hell in prison would be like.

AVIS. What a terrible thought – no more Dom Perringnon. And wearing those drab uniforms …

RICHARD. Not **prison** prison. **Prison** as in if I still had to work for Roger Cabot! But I just can't! I'm not cut out for all this back stabbing – literally. I'm a failure! Isn't it wonderful? But if Roger finds out, he's going to send me to Bali!

AVIS. Bali? Well, it really is a lovely place, Richard.

RICHARD. Not the **island** Bali!…He sent Paul McDougal there just because he wore a skirt!

AVIS. Then Roger is still alive?

RICHARD. The Anti-Christ's out on the patio, if you want to make sure.

AVIS. I only have one question.

RICHARD. What's that?

AVIS. *(speaking in a French accent)* What do you think he'll do when he hears you've been selling his paintings – eh, **Dante?**

RICHARD. *(surprised)* **You** were the French woman just now. *(with realization)* **You** were the French woman who phoned two weeks ago.

AVIS. Mais oui. *(sropping the accent)* It was obvious when I called, Roger didn't know anything about Dante Ruse. You on the other hand…

RICHARD. How did you find out?

AVIS. I didn't go to law school for nothing – I snooped through the gallery's files when the owner was distracted. Came up with the name Dante Ruse, records of payments. I just put two and two together. And I could help Roger do the same.

RICHARD. I suppose you want money to keep your mouth shut.

AVIS. Really! I'm not like everyone else, in case you hadn't noticed.

RICHARD. Then what do you want?

AVIS. I want you to still marry Rebecca. I've seen how she and Jason make goo-goo eyes at each other. Just do whatever it takes to ensure Roger will want *you* as his favorite son-in-law.

RICHARD. But – I can't!

AVIS. But you will! Unless you prefer – the tropics?

(The intercom BUZZES.)

RICHARD. *(to himself)* Thomas! *(to AVIS)* Quick – get in the bedroom.

AVIS. What?!

RICHARD. That's the gallery owner whose files you snooped through. And he *doesn't* know that I'm not Dante. So unless you want to blow any chance Roger will want me to marry Rebecca, you'll get in the bedroom.

(AVIS quickly exits into the bedroom, upstage left, closing the door behind her while RICHARD crosses to the intercom.)

(speaking into the intercom) Go away! We don't want any!

THOMAS. *(over the intercom)* Dante? Is that you?

(ROGER opens the French doors and drapes and stands in the doorway.)

RICHARD. Ah – *(seeing* **ROGER***, startled)* Ah!

ROGER. Well? Have you done it? Where's the body?

THOMAS. *(over the intercom)* It's me – Thomas. What's going on up there?

ROGER. How rude! You've been keeping him waiting this whole time, Richard.

THOMAS. *(over the intercom)* Will you please let me up?

ROGER. Do what the man says.

RICHARD. *(pressing the buzzer, speaking to himself about Thomas)* It's your funeral.

(There is a KNOCK on the door, downstage right.)

That can't be Thomas already.

ROGER. That's right. I invited Rebecca.

RICHARD. You don't want me to kill your daughter, too, do you?!

ROGER. *(crossing to open the door, downstage right)* Of course not. What do you take me for?

RICHARD. Oh, just a lunatic.

ROGER. *(opening the downstage right door, revealing* **REBECCA***)* Sweetheart, come in.

REBECCA. *(entering)* What is it, Dad? You sounded urgent on the phone.

ROGER. Nothing to get alarmed about. It's just that – well – I'm afraid I've been making some rather poor business decisions lately.

RICHARD. *(sarcastically)* Tell me about it.

ROGER. Yes – well – It seems I've lost everything.

REBECCA. Everything?

RICHARD. What exactly do you mean by "everything"?

ROGER. All my stocks. My bonds. The vacation home in the Caymans. It's all gone. Even the company is heavily in debt. I'm afraid there's nothing left.

RICHARD. Nothing left?

REBECCA. Dad, I'm so sorry. You worked so hard for all you had.

RICHARD. *(elated)* Nothing left? Thank God!

   *(**THOMAS** enters.)*

   *(to **REBECCA**)* If there's nothing left, then there's no reason to marry you!

THOMAS. A free man! At last!

AVIS. *(entering hurriedly from the bedroom, speaking in a warning tone)* Richard! Just because he's broke doesn't mean he still won't send you to Bali!

THOMAS. Who's Richard?

REBECCA. *(pointing to **RICHARD**)* He is.

THOMAS. *(to **RICHARD**)* But I thought you were Roger.

ROGER. *I'm* Roger.

THOMAS. *(to **ROGER**)* *You're* Roger? *(to **RICHARD**)* And you're *Richard*?…Are you still Dante, too?

ROGER. *(after a beat, slyly)* Well, Richard? Are you Dante?

RICHARD. *(after a tortured moment, suddenly animated and empowered with relief)* Yes! Yes! *I'm* Dante!

AVIS. Oh, crap!

RICHARD. And *I've* been selling your paintings and keeping the money! And I'm not going to shoot Adam Parnell! Or Thomas! So there!

THOMAS. Shoot – *who*?!

RICHARD. I don't want to be a part of your family! I don't want to be your heir apparent! I'm destined to be something other than a clone of Roger Cabot! I'll never be like you! Never! I'm so happy!

THOMAS. Shoot *who*?!

RICHARD. *(to **ROGER**)* And you're broke! And totally insane! *(tapping his head)* I think Jason must have fried a few wires up there.

AVIS. But you're still going to marry his daughter – right?

RICHARD. You really don't listen, do you? I just want to forget I ever knew the Cabot family. *(turning to **REBECCA**)* You don't really want to marry me, do you, Rebecca? You and I are really two completely different kinds of people with absolutely nothing in common.

AVIS. Is that any reason to call off the engagement?

*(**JASON** enters. He is dressed in khaki safari shirt and pants, an Indiana Jones hat, and hiking boots. A round, Indian drum is slung over his back.)*

*(at the sight of **JASON**)* My God! Why are you dressed like that?

JASON. This is me, Avis! The *real* me! I won't hide it any longer!

(He beats his drum and howls.)

ROGER. Just in time, Jason. I believe Richard and my daughter are about to become unengaged.

JASON. Unengaged? Is it really true?

RICHARD. The thing is, Rebecca, I don't know how to exactly explain this to you. I can hardly explain it to myself. I like you. You're very nice. But you're not my type. Can you understand?

REBECCA. I thought I wanted to marry you. You were just like Dad –

RICHARD. God, don't say that!

REBECCA. But the truth is, Richard – I could never marry someone like you.

RICHARD. Well, you don't have to be so honest!

THOMAS. *Who* did you say you were going to shoot?

RICHARD. I said I *wasn't* going to shoot you. So, let's not overreact.

JASON. So you're not going to marry Richard?

REBECCA. No. I'm not.

JASON. Because if you aren't – well –the thing is – I love –

(He reaches for her, but knocks over a stack of papers off the desk. Speaking as he hastily puts the papers back together and places them on the desk.)

Oh! I'm terribly sorry! It's just that – can't you see? I love –

AVIS. Jason! Aren't you forgetting something?

JASON. *(apologetically)* Oh, yes. You're right, Avis. Forgive me. What was I thinking?

(He gets down on one knee.)

I love you, Rebecca. Please run away with me!

AVIS. Jason! You're already engaged – to me! And I'm not going to give you up! Even if you do insist on dressing like that.

JASON. Even if I love someone else?

AVIS. What does that have to do with getting married?

REBECCA. Even if you weren't engaged to someone else, I could never marry someone who's done what you've done to my dad!

JASON. But I haven't done anything! He's the same man! *(pleading to* **ROGER***)* Roger? Tell them! Please!

REBECCA. Not the Shark! Not the Wolf of Wallstreet! I want the one who painted purple women. The one who saw a blue swirl with a touch of pink like a giant lollipop whenever he said my name. The dad who talked to me, who spent time with me, who grew to know me, to like me.

ROGER. Are you saying *that's* the dad you want?

REBECCA. Yes! And he's the dad I love!

ROGER. Rebecca – you don't know how long I've wanted you to say that.

RICHARD. Be careful what you wish for, Rebecca, you may get it.

ROGER. *(picking up the gun and aims it at* **RICHARD***)* And Richard – you don't know how long I've wanted to do this.

RICHARD.	**JASON.**	**REBECCA.**	**THOMAS.**
Sir?!	Roger!	Dad!	Ah!

(He fires.)

RICHARD. *(grabbing his chest and collapsing)* Ah!

THOMAS. *(rushing to* **RICHARD***'s side)* Dante! Darling!

RICHARD. *(looking at the palm of the hand that grabbed his chest)* Blood! He's shot me! I'm dying!

THOMAS. Speak to me!

RICHARD. *(speaking haltingly)* Thomas – you're the only one who ever understood me. Everything's going black…

THOMAS. *(examining the palm)* Richard –. Richard! It's paint.

RICHARD. Paint?

THOMAS. Cadmium Red.

ROGER. I loaded the gun with blanks before I gave it to you, Richard.

(One of the telephones RINGS. Then another RINGS.)

(wincing, holding up his hands in front of his eyes) Oh! Those horrible jagged reds and yellows!

*(Everyone except **JASON** stares at **ROGER** in surprise. **JASON** holds out his hand in a gesture of "What did I tell you?")*

Will someone please stop them!

RICHARD. You're *seeing* the *ringing*?! He's *seeing* the *ringing*!

*(**JASON** picks all the receivers off their cradles and places them on the desk.)*

You're not cured! You never *have* been cured!

ROGER. Always quick on the uptake, you were.

REBECCA. Dad? Is it really – you?

ROGER. It's really me. I never went through with the operation. Jason convinced me otherwise.

REBECCA. He did?

ROGER. Are you angry that I lied?

RICHARD. Well – yes! Do you know what kind of hell you put me through?

ROGER. I really did send Paul McDougal to Bali, Richard. *(picking up a manila envelope)* And if that doesn't shut you up, then I have some interesting photographs of you in – shall we say – evening attire?

THOMAS. *(quickly taking the envelope before* **RICHARD** *can)* I'd like a look at those.

RICHARD. Thomas! Give those back!

*(***THOMAS*** quickly exits onto the patio, with* **RICHARD** *following.)*

REBECCA. *(crosses to hug* **ROGER***)* I'm so glad you're back, Dad.

ROGER. I never left. Now, I believe Jason here asked you a question.

REBECCA. And I'm ready to answer him.

AVIS. Hello? Did everyone forget *I* was here?

ROGER. We try our best, but you keep speaking.

AVIS. Jason and I *will* be married – and no one is going to change that.

JASON. You're right, Avis. My commitment is to you.

REBECCA. It is?

AVIS. I'm always right. Everyone should know that by now.

JASON. Yes. Well, then, as my bride-to-be, you should know I'm getting rid of my Mercedes and Park Avenue condo.

AVIS. What do you mean you're getting rid of your Mercedes and Park Avenue condo?

JASON. Well, we won't need them where we're going.

AVIS. And just where are we going?

JASON. Off to the Guatemalan Rainforest!

AVIS. The Guatemalan Rainforest?!

JASON. Yes – there are these giant spiders there. I plan to study their venom.

AVIS. Giant spiders?! *(stealing herself)* That's not so bad.

ROGER. And piranha with all those flesh gnawing teeth.

REBECCA. And huge anacondas that can swallow you whole.

AVIS. Piranha?! Anacondas?! *(stealing herself)* I've handled worse in court.

ROGER. And no shopping.

AVIS. No shopping?! That's horrible!

JASON. Don't worry, Avis. You won't need much more than a loin cloth in that kind of heat. Think of it! It'll be just you and me – side by side – you holding each of those giant squirming spiders still while I extract the poison from its fangs.

AVIS. I'm sorry, Jason – the engagement is off.

JASON. But, Avis –

AVIS. Save it – I know when I've lost. But I'm going to keep the ring. *(to **ROGER**)* By the way – I assume since you're still nuts you'll keep painting?

ROGER. Nothing could stop me.

AVIS. *(crossing downstage right to depart)* Good. At least I've gotten something out of this mess. I just bought one of your paintings for $20,000.

ROGER. Really? So you've grown to like my work?

AVIS. God, no. It's an investment. The best thing you could do for me is to paint about fifty more and then drop dead.

(She begins to exit.)

ROGER. By the way – which painting did you buy?

AVIS. *Leda in Yellow.*

(She exits.)

ROGER. *(perplexed, to himself)* Leda in – **Yellow**?

*(with realization as he crosses to the French doors and gestures for **RICHARD** to come inside)*

Dante!

JASON. Rebecca –

REBECCA. Yes?

JASON. *(betting on one knee, taking her hand)* Will you marry me? I'll promise you the adventure of a lifetime.

REBECCA. No.

JASON. No? But remember? I *didn't* change your father.

REBECCA. I'm not ready to get married. Not even to you.

JASON. What can I do to change your mind?

(*She grabs him and kisses him passionately. He stumbles backwards.*)

Wow! Can we do that again?

(*They kiss passionately.*)

Does this mean yes?

REBECCA. No.

JASON. No?

REBECCA. Yes. But it does mean I'm ready for the adventure of a lifetime.

JASON. You are? With me?

REBECCA. With you. Living in the Guatemalan Rainforest, photographing all those giant spiders and anacondas and flesh-eating piranha! It sounds wonderful! I can't wait to begin exploring!

JASON. How about now?

(*They kiss passionately.*)

(**RICHARD** *and* **THOMAS** *appear in the French doorway.*)

ROGER. (*to* **RICHARD**) So you got $20,000 for *Leda in* **Yellow**?

RICHARD. *Twenty thousand dollars*?! Thomas – is it true?

THOMAS. (*presenting the check*) Here's the check –

ROGER. (*snatching the check*) I'll take that. Thank you.

RICHARD. (*snatching the check back*) *I* painted *Leda in Yellow*.

ROGER. (*snatching the check back*) But you still owe me for *Leda in Purple*.

RICHARD. (*snatching the check back*) That was *my* painting. You gave it to me if you recall!

REBECCA. But Richard, you said you detested it.

ROGER. Really?

(*He snatches the check back.*)

RICHARD. I never said the word "detest," Rebecca. Although I *do* detest it. But that's before I knew it was worth

$10,000.

(He snatches the check back.)

ROGER. *(to* **THOMAS***)* Ten thousand? How can an original Roger get a mere ten thousand and his fake – twenty? *(to* **RICHARD***, snatching the check back)* And what about the money you got for all my other paintings?

THOMAS. *Your* paintings? You mean – you really are Roger – the artist?

ROGER. He's cute, but he's slow, isn't he?

THOMAS. *(to* **RICHARD***)* But I saw you paint *Leda in Yellow* and *Leda in White* –

ROGER. *Leda in* **White**?! Just how many more *Ledas* are there?

RICHARD. Just *Leda in Red.*

THOMAS. What about the other paintings? I mean - the *non-Leda* paintings. Are they Roger forgeries, too?

ROGER. What other paintings?

THOMAS. The ones – Richard – I mean – Dante – I mean – the ones *he* painted.

ROGER. You painted non-*Leda* paintings, Richard?

RICHARD. Yes! Yes! I did it! None of that *Leda* crap! Do you hear? And Thomas loved them! Didn't you, Thomas? And they're *my* paintings! *Mine*! I'm alive! Alive! *I* am the one and true artist Dante!

ROGER. I'm so happy for you.

THOMAS. So am I, Dante.

ROGER. You can do what you want with your paintings, Dante. But you'll have to destroy all the fake *Ledas.*

THOMAS. Destroy them?! But you can't! They're master-pieces! The darlings of the art world! And at $20,000 a piece that's – *(calculating briefly)* $60,000!

RICHARD. I knew I kept you around for something.

ROGER. I said destroy them all – remember – I still have those photos of you –

THOMAS. *(feeling his breast pocket)* I thought I had them.

RICHARD. I've always hated those *Ledas*, anyway. It'll be my pleasure to destroy them.

ROGER. All except *Leda in Yellow*. I want Avis to have something that reminds her of me. When she tries to sell it, then we'll expose it as a fake. In the meantime, I'll paint some real *Ledas* for you, Thomas.

RICHARD. Thomas wants me, if you don't mind. Isn't that right, Thomas?

THOMAS. Oh yes! Shall we talk about your paintings – and other things – over dinner?

RICHARD. Let's see I've dressed up like a woman, nearly got arrested, agreed to kill myself, painted three hideous *Ledas*, and discovered I'm the artist Dante – Why not?

(RICHARD *and* THOMAS *exit, downstage right, arm in arm.*)

REBECCA. Dad – what did you mean about sending Paul McDougal to Bali? I saw him yesterday in the office.

ROGER. Did he have a tan?

REBECCA. Well – now that you mention it, he did.

ROGER. Well – there you go.

(ABIGAIL *appears in the doorway.*)

REBECCA. What will you do now that you've lost all your money, Dad?

ROGER. Don't worry. I'll be ok. I still have my loft – and my paintings aren't doing too badly, either.

JASON. (*sweeping* REBECCA *into his arms*) Well, we have lots of plans to make! (*running into* ABIGAIL *as they start to exit, downstage right*) Abigail! Rebecca and I are off to live with giant spiders and snakes in the Guatemalan Rainforest! Isn't it wonderful!

ABIGAIL. Now that's true love.

(REBECCA *and* JASON *exit with* REBECCA *beating Jason's drum.*)

ROGER. I thought you weren't coming back.

ABIGAIL. I wasn't. I just came to say good-bye. Well – good-bye.

(She starts to exit, downstage right.)

ROGER. You didn't come all this way just to say good-bye.

ABIGAIL. *(turning toward him, upset)* You are such a know-it-all!

ROGER. I know.

ABIGAIL. You are so difficult!

ROGER. I know.

ABIGAIL. You are impossible!

ROGER. I know, Abigail – like warm caramel half moons melting on my tongue ...

ABIGAIL. *(with realization that he never had become the "old" Roger)* You bastard!

ROGER. You shouldn't have deceived me. A man never forgets that sort of thing.

ABIGAIL. But does he forgive?

ROGER. The earth did rumble, Abigail.

ABIGAIL. I know. It's rumbling still.

ROGER. Have you ever been to Bali? It's an island of artists and incredible beauty.

ABIGAIL. But didn't I just overhear Rebecca say you've lost everything?

ROGER. I may be crazy, but I'm not stupid. I still have a little bungalow there. I want to paint you in the nude with a purple orchid in your hair. And you could write that great American novel. *(moving toward her)* So what do you want to do?

ABIGAIL. *(moving toward him)* I'll let you know when we get there.

(RAPID FADE to BLACK.)

End of Play

PRODUCTION NOTES

- The sculpture chair "Millennium's End: Seating for None" should resemble a chair; however, it should be very difficult to actually sit on in a normal way. *(See illustration of sculpture chair used in the staged reading performed at New England Academy of Theatre.*
- The "Leda" of the paintings is pronounced LEE-da, as in "Leda and the Swan."
- Avis Harpinger's last name is pronounced HARP-in-jer.
- Synesthesia is a real neurological "condition" in which two senses are cross-wired. Roger, in Act I, should openly react to some of the more distinctive sounds. In Act II, he should still react, but so that his reactions aren't apparent to anyone except Jason and the audience.

PROPERTY PLOT

Top of Show Preset

UPSTAGE: various large canvases stacked against the wall.
UR: large easel with large canvas, stool, small table with oil paints, two jars, a coffee can containing paintbrushes.
UC: mobile of crystals near French doors, plain drapes on either side of the French doors
UC, ON PATIO: tape deck
DC: Sculpture chair covered with cloth; low, narrow, black table or armless and backless bench; various throw pillows scattered on the floor.
IN DL KITCHEN AREA: tape deck.

PROP TABLE, DR:

ABIGAIL: beeper, notepad, pen, file folder containing papers
JASON cell phone
THOMAS: business card
AVIS: briefcase

PROP TABLE, UL:

ROGER: easel, small table with paint supplies, large canvas

Intermission preset

STRIKE:
All paintings; all furniture, including the ottoman, the throw pillows, the sculpture chair, the cover, the easels, the stools, the small tables; all painting supplies, the tape decks.

SET:
UC: decorative drapes on either side of the French doors.
UR: a small office chair

UL: an imposing office chair and a huge desk with a computer, several telephones and stacks of paper, a small note pad, a pen

NEXT TO THE DESK: a shopping bag containing a sexy, red satin dress, a blonde wig and a pair of spike heels

KITCHEN AREA: a tea kettle, a wooden spoon, a bottle of Perrier in the refrigerator

PROP TABLE, DR:

RICHARD: two suits on hangers in dry cleaning bags, a briefcase.
REBECCA: purse containing business-sized check

From II-1 to II-2
SET:
OVER BACK OF CHAIR, UL: Roger's pants
DESK DRAWER: handgun

PROP TABLE, DR:

RICHARD: small purse containing cell phone

From II-2 to II-3
STRIKE: Wig
SET:
ON UR DESK: manila envelope with large black and white photographs

PROP TABLE, DR

RICHARD: handgun
JASON: Indian drum
THOMAS: check

Killing Dante set

city skyline

patio

large, artistic rock formation

industrial windows

industrial windows

French doors

modern sculpture

door to bedroom/bath

kitchen area

paintings

throw pillows

ottoman

sculpture chair

easel, stool, and small table

paintings

door to building hall

Downstage

OTHER TITLES AVAILABLE FROM SAMUEL FRENCH

THE OFFICE PLAYS
Two full length plays by Adam Bock

THE RECEPTIONIST
Comedy / 2m., 2f. Interior

At the start of a typical day in the Northeast Office, Beverly deals effortlessly with ringing phones and her colleague's romantic troubles. But the appearance of a charming rep from the Central Office disrupts the friendly routine. And as the true nature of the company's business becomes apparent, The Receptionist raises disquieting, provocative questions about the consequences of complicity with evil.

"...Mr. Bock's poisoned Post-it note of a play." - *New York Times*

"Bock's intense initial focus on the routine goes to the heart of
The Receptionist's pointed, painfully timely allegory... elliptical,
provocative play..."
- *Time Out New York*

THE THUGS
Comedy / 2m, 6f / Interior

The Obie Award winning dark comedy about work, thunder and the mysterious things that are happening on the 9th floor of a big law firm. When a group of temps try to discover the secrets that lurk in the hidden crevices of their workplace, they realize they would rather believe in gossip and rumors than face dangerous realities.

"Bock starts you off giggling, but leaves you with a chill."
- *Time Out New York*

"... a delightfully paranoid little nightmare that is both more
chillingly realistic and pointedly absurd than anything
John Grisham ever dreamed up."
- *New York Times*